Melbourne-born author Geoff McGeachin started his working life as a photographer, shooting pictures for advertising, travel, theatre and feature films. His career has taken him all over the world, including stints living in Los Angeles, New York and Hong Kong. He is now based in Sydney, taking pictures, teaching photography and writing.

Geoff's first novel, *Fat, Fifty & F***ed!*, won the inaugural Australian Popular Fiction Competition. His third book, *Sensitive New Age Spy*, continues the adventures of special agent Alby Murdoch.

By the same author

Fat, Fifty & F***ed!
Sensitive New Age Spy

GEOFF McGEACHIN

D-E-D Dead!

PENGUIN BOOKS

DED-icated with much love to the inspirational and wickedly funny Wilma Schinella; creative consultant, muse, amuse-gueule and editor of first and last resort. She helps to make this writing caper fun.

PENGUIN BOOKS

Published by the Penguin Group
Penguin Group (Australia)
250 Camberwell Road, Camberwell, Victoria 3124, Australia
(a division of Pearson Australia Group Pty Ltd)
Penguin Group (USA) Inc.
375 Hudson Street, New York, New York 10014, USA
Penguin Group (Canada)
90 Eglinton Avenue East, Suite 700, Toronto, Canada ON M4P 2Y3
(a division of Pearson Penguin Canada Inc.)
Penguin Books Ltd
80 Strand, London WC2R 0RL England
Penguin Ireland
25 St Stephen's Green, Dublin 2, Ireland
(a division of Penguin Books Ltd)
Penguin Books India Pvt Ltd
11 Community Centre, Panchsheel Park, New Delhi – 110 017, India
Penguin Group (NZ)
67 Apollo Drive, Rosedale, North Shore 0632, New Zealand
(a division of Pearson New Zealand Ltd)
Penguin Books (South Africa) (Pty) Ltd
24 Sturdee Avenue, Rosebank, Johannesburg 2196, South Africa

Penguin Books Ltd, Registered Offices: 80 Strand, London, WC2R 0RL, England

First published by Penguin Group (Australia), 2005
This edition published by Penguin Group (Australia), 2008

1 3 5 7 9 10 8 6 4 2

Text copyright © Geofrrey McGeachin 2005

The moral right of the author has been asserted

All rights reserved. Without limiting the rights under copyright reserved above, no part of this publication may be reproduced, stored in or introduced into a retrieval system, or transmitted, in any form or by any means (electronic, mechanical, photocopying, recording or otherwise), without the prior written permission of both the copyright owner and the above publisher of this book.

Cover and text design by Debra Billson © Penguin Group (Australia)
Cover illustration by Mark Sofilas
Typeset in 12.5/19 pt ITC Legacy Serif Book by Post Pre-press Group, Brisbane, Queensland
Printed and bound in Australia by McPherson's Printing Group, Maryborough, Victoria

National Library of Australia
Cataloguing-in-Publication data:

McGeachin, Geoffrey.
D-e-d dead!
ISBN 978 0 14 300423 3.
I. Title.

A823.4

penguin.com.au

ONE

I should have known it was going to be a lousy week when I dropped my gun in the tram on the way to the office. I guess I was a bit tired and edgy and concerned about being away from the action for so long. You miss being in the thick of things for the first few weeks and then you start wondering if you really miss it at all. Maybe I was getting too old for this spying lurk. What I really truly wanted was to be parked in a cane chair on a mountaintop somewhere in Bali, sipping a G and T and luxuriating in the serenity of a tropical paradise, instead of sitting like a gig on a Melbourne tram with my gun on the floor.

The unfortunate firearms incident occurred as the No. 16 W Class was rattling down a sun-dappled St Kilda Road scattering crisp early-autumn leaves and blue-blazered, backpack-toting public schoolboys from its path. The geriatric Ws, vintage trams with a pedigree going back to the thirties, had been withdrawn from service a few years ago when they began exhibiting a distinct lack of interest in responding to the brakes. After a lot of grousing from the public, and a multi-million-dollar refit, fifty or so of these boxy veterans were now back on the rails for the benefit of tourists and nostalgia freaks. Only in Melbourne would commuters with a fleet of sleek European-style trams at their disposal demand the return of these damp, draughty, uncomfortable and noisy relics.

Foibles like these, plus the wide streets and excellent restaurants, help to make Melbourne one of Australia's great cities. For my money though, you only want to live in Melbourne a couple of months of the year, and it was getting towards the end of those months. This was definitely an autumn-and-spring kind of town. The lung-blistering dry heat of summer was long gone and the abject misery of another wet, cold, depressing winter was looming. There was a very good reason why out-of-towners like me called the joint 'Bleak City'. The grey chill of the long winter, compounded by the locals' fanatical devotion to Australian Rules Football, made me glad my three-month posting was almost over and I would soon be escaping back north to a more temperate and less sports-mad Sydney. In Sydney no-one really cared if your parents hadn't sworn a blood oath of lifelong dedication to one particular football team on your behalf within seconds of your birth.

It was right on 9 a.m. when we crossed the Princes Bridge

and rattled past the Arts Centre and the National Gallery. You don't often see a W Class on the City to St Kilda route and I was enjoying the ride, right up to the second when we reached the Domain interchange. Only moments before, the ticket inspector – or to give him his official title, Revenue Protection Officer – had decided to start earning his keep. As I leaned forward to get the ticket from my wallet in my back trouser pocket the tram hit the interchange points where the tracks split off towards the Botanical Gardens. There was a metallic squeal from the wheels, then a jolt and the little Sauer 9mm semi-automatic made a slow-motion swan dive out of my shoulder holster. The weapon thudded onto the ribbed wooden floor, smack bang at the feet of the scruffy young Yarra Trams employee. He stared gloomily down at the battered blue steel pistol resting between the scuffed toes of his Doc Martens.

'Youse aren't supposed to have a gun on a tram,' he said. And then, after a pause, 'That a valid ticket?'

Strictly speaking you're not supposed to carry a pistol anywhere in the country. The general exceptions are on-duty police officers, licensed security guards, media magnates and their bodyguards, and all those Wyatt Earps who belong to pistol clubs. And technically they're only supposed to carry firearms on the shortest possible route between the club's shooting range and their homes. It's a funny thing how often that route seems to take in pubs, 7-Eleven parking lots, seedy dance clubs and all the other places dickheads and smart alecs like to congregate.

'It's just a replica,' I said loudly for the benefit of several alert and very alarmed-looking fellow passengers. 'Birthday present for my nephew.'

Flashing the phoney police ID card that went with the gun seemed to satisfy the ticket inspector. The name on the card, Alby Murdoch, was mine, as was the face in the photo, but I was carrying a lot less bottle age when the picture was taken. A cheap trick like that wouldn't have worked in the old days, before privatisation and automatic ticket machines, when female conductors ran Melbourne's trams like private fiefdoms. An old-style connie with a hand-knitted cardigan under her cigarette-ash-dusted Melbourne Metropolitan Tramways Board blue woollen blazer would have given me a real earbashing. Probably would have confiscated the pistol too. I'm pretty sure that there was a Directorate regulation somewhere that said you could never, ever justify losing your weapon except if a MMTB connie took it off you and wouldn't give it back. Never push your luck with a Melbourne connie was the rule. Back then even real cops were wary of them.

Be that as it may, by this time I was much more interested in the raven-haired woman sitting opposite me who had very kindly bent down to retrieve my gun. She was thirtyish, I guessed, and fairly attractive, in a jaw-droppingly gorgeous kind of way – tall, great legs in sleek stockings, beautifully tailored suit, thin and expensive-looking briefcase and a disarming smile. And olive skin, great cheekbones and the most extraordinary slate-grey eyes. Being a spy made me notice the details; being a photographer made me appreciate them. Plus, of course, I'm a bloke.

'Aren't you a little too old to be playing with toys?' she asked. She had quite a sparkle in those grey eyes. The accent was definitely American, her nails were perfectly manicured and I almost missed the movement as her thumb casually checked the safety catch before she handed me the pistol, butt first, muzzle down. Which, of course, was exactly the right way to do it, according to my small-arms instructor in basic weapons training in spy school, way back when. The woman pulled the cord and got off at the next stop, one before mine.

Now this was certainly a turn-up for the books; two people perched opposite each other on the slippery wooden seats of the No. 16 City to St Kilda W Class who both knew how to handle a shooter. What the hell was genteel old Melbourne coming to?

TWO

The WORLDPIX head office was still sitting right where I'd put it all those years ago. That was one thing about Melbourne: when someone whacks up a building it tends to stay put. Turn your back on some familiar office tower in Sydney and the next time you look it's either a great big hole in the ground or something new, taller, bolder and brasher.

St Kilda Road is a wide, almost European boulevard that was once known for its trees, trams and elegant mansions. It still has the trams and the trees but the mansions disappeared a long time ago, making way for row upon row of steel and glass towers, many of which house advertising agencies. In general, ad agency executives are decrepit and dissolute old lechers and they like to window-dress their front offices with incredibly beautiful and nubile young women. I'd suggested to the planning committee that we locate our offices in one of these mirrored towers since it was great cover, and made perfect sense as we'd be doing a lot of business with the advertising world. And as for riding up and down in the elevators around midday or at knocking-off time . . . well, that was a bit of a bonus.

The head office of WORLDPIX INTERNATIONAL PHOTO-AGENCY NL occupies the whole of the twelfth floor and it looks very, very slick, which befits our status as one of the leading suppliers of photographic images worldwide. Lots of chrome and glass and leather and even the filing cabinets and light boxes are top quality – our clients expect that and God knows we charge them enough for the rights to use our photographs. The smaller magazines and ad agencies sometimes complain bitterly but we've never been known to drop our prices. When you deal with WORLDPIX you're dealing with the best and you know right from the word go that it's going to cost you.

The business cards in my wallet, next to the phoney police ID, identified me as WORLDPIX's senior international photographer. One of my favourite shots, taken in Afghanistan in the early eighties, was hanging in the twelfth-floor foyer, opposite the elevator: a two by three metre full-colour blow-up of a magnificent Markhor mountain goat standing regally on a rocky outcrop with the sun breaking over the peaks of the Hindu Kush behind him. That photograph had been the catalyst for bringing WORLDPIX into existence and it always gave me a bit of a buzz when I saw it.

Once past the giant photograph, you come to our multi-lingual and rather spunky receptionist Nhu and then the office temporarily occupied by the lovely Julie. Julie is about thirty, which to my mind is an excellent age, has long blonde hair, a killer smile and a mind like a steel trap. Julie usually runs our Sydney office but was down in Melbourne filling in for someone who was due back soon from maternity leave.

Julie can take real shorthand, type ninety words a minute and schedule a five-continents-in-ten-days photographic shoot so it goes off without a hitch. As well, she handles the complicated balancing act of running the day-to-day public operations of WORLDPIX and seamlessly integrating them with the other, less well-known work we do.

Julie can also break your heart with a shake of her head and your arm with a flick of her wrist. I'd had a bit of the former and none of the latter and right now we were working hard on just being good friends.

'Maybe you should look at your watch once in a while,' she said, glancing up from her computer screen. 'You Know Who wants to see you, pronto.'

The spy game depends on cryptic and intriguing messages like this to keep its allure. 'You Know Who' was my boss, Gordon Dalkeith.

'So a quick knee-trembler in the stationery cupboard's out of the question then?'

'Don't dick around, Alby,' she said, 'he's in one of his moods and he's got Shit for Brains in with him.'

'Shit for Brains' was Julie's affectionate nickname for Sheldon Asher, the Sydney-based CIA Station Head in

Australia. He and Gordon had become best buddies over the last couple of years. It was like their own little coalition of the willing.

'If there's even the remotest chance of encountering Sheldon and Gordon together in the same room,' I said, 'then I shall of course fly swiftly, as if on wingéd feet.'

She shook her head and gave me a pitying look.

Once safely past Julie's lustful clutches and the rows of filing cabinets and offices full of high-end computers and our busy image sales staff, you come to the area marked FILM PROCESSING SECTION. There's just a blank wall and a single very solid-looking door with a red light mounted over it. The sign on the door reads DARKROOMS – DO NOT ENTER WHEN RED LIGHT IS ON. The red light is always on and the door is blast-proof, so you'd need an anti-tank gun or two hours with a diamond-tipped drill to get in and ruin our happy snaps. I stood in front of the video-camera lens concealed under the red light and smiled. Benny buzzed me in through the security door.

I walked down a matt black painted corridor that loops back on itself as a light trap, then followed a trail of dim green lights on the floor past the clanking and gurgling film processors. The processors gurgle and clank day and night but not a lot of film goes through nowadays. Mostly we shoot digital but the darkroom story justifies blocking off half the floor space and helps hide WORLDPIX's nasty little secret. The thirteenth floor.

I continued up the steel stairs at the rear of the darkrooms. Like a lot of high-rise office towers, our building officially has no thirteenth floor, to cater to the superstitious. Physically the thirteenth floor exists but the public elevators don't stop there and there are no windows. The thirteenth floor houses the offices of D-E-D or the Directorate for Extra-territorial Defence.

D-E-D is an ultra-secret government department tasked with providing diverse intelligence-gathering services for the Commonwealth of Australia. It came into existence during World War II as a support section for the network of coast-watchers who stayed behind when the Japanese occupied nearly every coral atoll between Brisbane and Yokohama. D-E-D was just a basic pack-and-ship-by-submarine supply service until a politically astute senior army officer had cunningly and unofficially transformed it into a covert photographic intelligence-gathering department. By running the operation lean and staying well out of the political spotlight, he'd managed to keep D-E-D going beyond the war's end and right up to his retirement in the sixties.

Those of us employed at the pointy end of all this intelligence gathering referred to ourselves as dedheads. I think Julie may have come up with the nickname and I'm not entirely sure it was meant to be complimentary.

Benny, our soon-to-be-superannuated security supervisor, sat at the surveillance station at the top of the stairs with his wall of video monitors, a cup of tea and some public-service biscuits. Twenty-three flickering screens showed varying angles of the twelfth floor, the underground car park, the main and rear building entrances, the fire escape and each of the elevators. The twenty-fourth screen was playing the home shopping channel and Benny was on the phone ordering a set of knives guaranteed to cut through tin cans, shoe leather and tomatoes for the rest of his life.

'Morning, Ben,' I said. 'Planning on filleting some elephants in our retirement, are we?'

His mumbled reply came mixed in a spray of biscuit crumbs. I signed the 'In' book and noticed the yellow action slip with my name on it. Apparently Gordon really did want to see me immediately. It was stamped 'Priority – Soonest' to indicate it was urgent, so naturally I popped it in the nearest shredder and headed down the corridor to the tearoom to make a cup of coffee.

The thirteenth floor is always busy. In Audio/Video, boffins were hunched over their computers, decoding microburst transmissions relayed in pauses in seemingly innocuous recorded interviews, or breaking up digital images of a royal wedding in Europe to extract encoded data on missing nuclear material from former Soviet-bloc countries.

In Camera Prep, Graeme Rutherford was checking camera bodies, lenses and laptops before carefully packing them into the airtight Pelican cases we use for overseas assignments. Graeme was old-school and hated the fact we mostly used digital instead of film now. He was a former field agent who had a nervous twitch and no fingernails, the legacy of an extended discussion on the merits of very long telephoto lenses with a bunch of secret policemen in the Shah's Iran in the old days. On the rare occasions he talked about it Graeme referred to his torturers as 'the gentlemen from SAVAK', which I thought was extremely generous of him given the circumstances.

The laminex table in the staff tearoom was scattered with morning papers trumpeting the recent upsurge in drugs, guns and violent crime. It was starting to look like the nation was in the middle of a full-blown epidemic. Hard to believe, but it had even managed to force football off the front page.

'Something Must Be Done!' screamed the *Herald Sun*'s editorial.

'Law and Order Crisis' bellowed *The Australian*.

'Breakdown of Civilised Values' roared *The Age*.

Tell me about it. When I looked in the cupboard I realised someone had been pinching my AllPress Special Dark Roast beans. This day kept getting worse. I managed to find enough beans in the grinder to coax a reasonable latte out of the Gaggia espresso machine. Life is way too short to drink instant coffee.

THREE

'Had any postcards from your mum?' I asked.

I only did it because I knew it drove him crazy. Gordon didn't like anyone bringing up his family, and especially not his mum. He might have worn Savile Row suits and had weekly manicures but the truth was Gordon came from a long line of Scottish socialists. The Dalkeiths were wharfies and union men right back to the year dot. It was probably a Dalkeith who cast off the ropes for Noah. The family had migrated to Australia in the fifties when Gordon was just a youngster, and he'd worked hard on eliminating all traces of the working-class Gorbals district of Glasgow and the Clyde shipyards from his speech. Unlike the rest of the Dalkeith clan Gordon's accent was now more Prince Charles than Billy Connolly.

When Gordon's widowed mum Dulcie found out he'd been recruited by the Department straight out of university in '68, she not only washed her hands of him but also defected to the Soviets. It wasn't quite as dramatic as it sounded, of course. She'd actually done a bunk from a *Women's Weekly* Romantic Eastern Europe Tour with a husky Hungarian tour guide and they were still shacked up together somewhere in Budapest.

Harry, my sometimes offsider, had met the woman once and it was his opinion that if it was a honey trap there was one Hungarian intelligence officer with an Order of Lenin First Class, and very well deserved. Must have been true love though, because when Soviet-style communism finally fell over Dulcie Dalkeith had shown absolutely no interest in moving back to the west, or West Melbourne to be precise. At the time of her defection the department hadn't been all that fussed; Dulcie Dalkeith was certainly no intelligence coup. She didn't know anything. Apparently it ran in the family. Gordon Dalkeith was so thick there was naturally only one job suitable for him in the service.

'I'm in charge of this department,' he said, 'and when I say I want you, I want you *now*. Do you understand?'

I nodded and sipped my coffee. Things were really getting grim. The same bastard who was nicking my coffee had also taken the last of the Orange Slice biscuits. Had Ben been eating Orange Slices? Perhaps if I managed to surreptitiously gather up some crumbs from his desk the boffins in R and D could identify them. After all, what's the point of having an ionising gas spectrometer in the cupboard if you can't use it to help out your mates occasionally?

Sheldon Asher was sitting on the couch in the corner

of Gordon's office wearing his usual outfit – the full Ralph Lauren Fall Collection accented with exquisite autumn tonings. The plaited leather bolo tie at his neck and the brown suede rippled-sole desert boots were the only jarring touches. When the bodgie gangs first wore those boots in the fifties they were nicknamed 'Brothel Creepers' and both the footwear and the moniker suited Sheldon to a T.

Sheldon was one of those teflon-coated political appointees from some long-past cowboy administration in Washington, and his posting down-under seemed to be going on for an indecently long time. The CIA either really wanted him on station in Australia or really, really didn't want him back at head office in Langley. You had to wonder exactly how many dirty little secrets he was keeping in his filing cabinet.

I'd been unofficially briefed on Sheldon before he arrived in Australia. The outgoing CIA Station Head, Kelly Moskowitz, had downed one too many bourbons at his farewell knees-up and let everything out.

'Sheldon might seem like one cold son of a bitch,' he'd slurred, 'but believe me, he's got the heart of a child.'

'Really?' I said, even though I knew what was coming.

'Yep,' Kelly continued with a grin. 'Bastard keeps it in a jar of formaldehyde on his desk.'

Sheldon, I later discovered, actually kept a jar of those tiny little jelly beans on his desk, but I knew exactly what Kelly had meant. And recently, besides being an over-stayer, Sheldon had become something of a name-dropper and a bit of a society gadabout, which was odd behaviour for a top spy.

Julie, who had the most amazing range of contacts, had told me there were also rumours he'd secretly bought into The Ice Chest, one of the hot nightspots in Kings Cross, as part of a long-term retirement strategy. The Ice Chest had a colourful history and had long been a haunt of Sydney's underworld heavies. According to the local wallopers it had also recently become known as the easiest place in town to stock up on ecstasy or crystal meth. If the rumour was true you'd have to wonder why something like that hadn't rung any alarm bells at CIA headquarters.

'Hey buddy boy,' Sheldon said, 'how're they hanging?'

I didn't like Sheldon Asher a whole lot. He was one of those people who kept talking about win/win situations. What a dickhead. People who hammer on about bloody win/win situations really get on my wick. Whatever happened to that perfectly acceptable word 'compromise'? And I also didn't think the current state of my testicles was any of his beeswax.

'Sheldon,' I said with a nod, and left it at that.

'Was there anything else, Shel?' Gordon asked, closing the file on his desk.

Sheldon shook his head and got up. About my age, he was fit and tanned and stood around five-foot-six. He claimed to be five-eight, which he was more than happy to tell you was average height. Maybe amongst the Kalahari bushmen.

Julie was prone to saying Sheldon compensated for his lack of height with his lack of personality. Very astute judge of character, our Jules.

'I'll take care of everything exactly as we discussed,' Sheldon said to Gordon with a smile. 'And I'll see you on the flip side, buddy boy,' he said to me with a wink.

'Not if I see you first,' I said, returning the wink.

It was a schoolyard response and I was ever so slightly ashamed of myself. Luckily Gordon's phone rang and made an embarrassing moment only awkward. After Sheldon had left I studied the cup and saucer on the coffee table in front of the couch where he'd been sitting. There were biscuit crumbs on the saucer. Orange crumbs. Bastard!

FOUR

Gordon reached across his desk and picked up the handset of the green phone. The green phone is one down from the red phone and one up from the black one. The Prime Minister always rings on the red one. I usually ring on the black one but more often than not Gordon wouldn't take my calls. He didn't like me much and it was certainly a two-way street.

He listened intently to the voice on the phone for a moment. 'Bad time, Buzz, let me call you back,' he said and hung up.

First Sheldon and now someone named Buzz. Gordon was taking the US–Australia alliance very seriously this morning.

'Did the commission cheque on my photographs come through yet?' I asked, after Gordon leaned back in his chair.

'What cheque?' he asked. 'Your salary?' He was confused; nothing new or terribly remarkable in that.

'The commission on sales of my photos,' I said. 'You owe me nine thousand bucks for March. Thanks to my superb entrepreneurial ability and visual acuity this is the only government department in the entire world that's totally self-supporting, so the least you could do is get my cheques out on time.'

In reality this was a bit of an understatement. Though theoretically operating only to provide cover for D-E-D, I knew WORLDPIX actually turned a substantial profit that went straight into the federal government's consolidated revenue pool, without attribution naturally.

WORLDPIX has stringers all over the globe, real photographers shooting real snaps for photo-hungry real clients: newspapers, magazines, book publishers and so on. We've also got offices in London, New York, Berlin and Tokyo and a very cool website showcasing our wares. All of it totally legit and all of it highly profitable. Ninety per cent of our photographers and one hundred per cent of our non-government customers have no idea of our real job. I'd always maintained Gordon Dalkeith fitted neatly into the latter category too.

We didn't get on all that well since he wasn't a spy or a photographer and in reality he wasn't even much of a department head. And WORLDPIX was my creation so I did feel a touch proprietorial towards it.

Gordon was still confused by my query about the cheque and so he did what every government department head does in a situation like this. He moved on.

'What are you and Wardell working on right now?' he asked.

My temporary Melbourne posting was to force me to tidy up the loose ends on my Master's, which had recently become compulsory for all senior operatives. How weird was that? Spies with degrees? But you couldn't work for the government now without the appropriate academic credentials, no matter what your job. The photojournalism BA I'd done in the US in the eighties had been fine for a long time but for any internal promotion nowadays you needed at least a Master's.

The snot-nosed punks breathing down my neck for the upper-level management positions had no pointy-end experience but they did have all the right academic qualifications. Since my days as a field operative would soon be over I'd been sweating out a Master's to try to keep ahead of the little bastards. The title of my just completed thesis, 'A Study of the Pre-emptive Use of Weapons of Mass Destruction in Occupied Palestine', had scored me many brownie points until Gordon actually sat down and read an early draft and discovered I was covering the introduction of the Ballista, or giant catapult, to the urban battlefield. The occupying forces under discussion were the Roman legions commanded by General Titus laying siege to Jerusalem in 70 AD.

Gordon was so pissed off that he'd lumbered me with a crummy assignment to make up for all the money D-E-D had spent on keeping me in town. Walking over to his desk I snapped on the computer, selected 'agent status', punched in my ID number and watched the display start flashing. Then a computer-generated voice began squawking from the speakers.

'Restricted – Station Head Only,' it bleated. *'Enter access code. Enter code within twenty seconds to avoid general alert.'*

A general alert was seriously noisy, involving klaxons going off, blast-proof steel shutters clanging down and our valiant security staff running about grasping cups of tea in one hand and vintage shooters that haven't been fired or cleaned in ten years in the other. A general alert was very dangerous to everyone involved and it was universally agreed that it was something best avoided at all cost.

'Want me to punch in your access code, Gordon?' I asked.

He smirked at this ludicrous idea so I typed in 'Mahler', which opened the file and silenced the squawking voice. That wiped the smile off his face.

'Well there you go,' I said, reading off the screen. 'As you ordered, Harry and I are doing the biannual positive vetting on US personnel at Bitter Springs. Why, I don't know, since I keep on telling you that it's a complete waste of time and it should be an ASIO gig anyway.'

The Springs are a massive US intelligence gathering facility in the dead heart of central Australia. Satellite dishes, radar domes and God knows what else, all enclosed inside electric fences and razor wire to keep out the skinks and dingoes. Of all the well-known top-secret US bases in Australia the Springs had always been the least well-known. Even the anti-base protesters couldn't find it until that black afternoon in the mid-eighties when a cheery Soviet Embassy press briefing on likely nuclear targets in this country gave out the complete address, including the postcode and nearest cross street.

In the heated days of the old Cold War the bods at the Springs were guaranteed a first or retaliatory multiple missile strike by at least six SS-18 Model 6 Satans fired out of the ICBM silos at Dombarovsky by valiant Soviet *rocketchiki*. One of the Russian boffins had mournfully predicted a ground temperature of five hundred thousand degrees Centigrade at the peak of a one hundred and twenty megaton attack like that. Harry Wardell, shooting the briefing publicly for WORLDPIX and sniffing around privately for D-E-D, had succinctly summed it up for the assembled press pack.

'If you need to pop outside during a thermonuclear event of this nature, be sure to wear a hat and sunglasses. And SPF two zillion sunblock.'

Harry was what is known in the trade as a funny bugger.

The Springs were officially classified as a US–Australian Joint Defence Facility, which translates as a facility on our sovereign territory staffed and run by the American National Security Agency for their own purposes and into which the landlord is not invited. The NSA is responsible for the extremely sophisticated electronic eavesdropping network that circles the globe and is answerable only to the highest levels of the American government.

We do have complete on-site over-sight of course, which apparently translates in Canberra-speak as two career-stalled, middle-ranking defence force officers locked in a small windowless room with a DVD player, a widescreen TV and all the stewed coffee and air-freighted Krispy Kreme donuts they can handle. Every couple of years, to maintain this pathetic illusion that we actually have some control over the Springs, the Australian government carries out a security exercise to check on the bona fides of all these mysterious Americans working inside the base.

'And how is the vetting coming along?' Gordon asked. He was still trying to regain his composure after my little trick with his computer access code.

'Just great,' I said.

In actual fact I didn't really know since I'd flick-passed the whole pointless exercise to Harry. He was working in the Sydney office and we'd tried sorting things out over a secure computer link but it was an almost impossible task to coordinate from two different locations. It had become a real pain for an assignment nobody gave two hoots about anyway.

The vetting was really a one-man job but Harry had been roped into helping me as punishment for surreptitiously releasing a shot he'd snapped of the Prime Minister possibly picking his nose. When it finally became obvious that we were both doing the same thing in different cities Harry had offered to take on the whole job himself. It was his way of paying back a favour I'd done him last New Year's Eve when

I'd worked his shift in the Sydney office. I missed out on the fireworks spectacular over the Harbour but the swap allowed Harry to generate his own fireworks with one of the girls from International Billing.

Harry taking over the whole Springs assignment also meant I had more time to spend on my thesis and we decided Gordon didn't really need to know about our arrangement. And since these vetting-the-Yanks things always tended to follow the same path I felt fairly confident in telling Gordon a fib.

'As usual the CIA have handed over a list of three hundred names and dates of birth and refused us access to all other records, information and data,' I said. 'If we can't find Joseph Stalin or Vladimir Putin's name on the list we'll just have to pass them all as 100 per cent USDA Prime, bona fide all-American boys. Like we do every damned time. Where are you keeping the rubber stamp this week?'

The irony was lost on Gordon. He actually seemed to believe in the 'special relationship'. They screw us and if we keep very quiet about it our Prime Minister is invited to Washington every couple of years. He gets to watch a lot of square-jawed, ramrod-straight and neatly pressed soldiers march up and down and then profusely thank the President and a gaggle of hangers-on at a gala dinner. It seems to work out well for everyone, even if they usually get the PM's name wrong on the wire services.

'We want you in Hong Kong for the Dragon Boat Races,'

Gordon said. 'You leave tomorrow. I'm putting Wardell on another project. The vetting can wait.'

'Just the race or is there something else?' I asked. I liked Honkers and I'd spent a year there once, running our local office. But Hong Kong was now back in Chinese hands and we had to watch our footwork. Not anywhere near as much fun as the old days when the ex-pat senior police were on our side and the chef at the Great Shanghai restaurant in Tsim Sha Tsui could be relied on for a feast of succulent stir-fried Shanghai freshwater hairy crab and sautéed snow pea sprouts at four in the morning after some cross-border chicanery.

Gordon shook his head. 'This trip's just to maintain your cover,' he said, 'since you've had a low profile lately. And to top up the library. Some of the Hong Kong shots on file are getting a bit dated.'

That's the thing about a photo-library in this visually literate electronic age; the older snaps really tend to stick out. But at least it was an assignment. It would get me on a plane somewhere and Hong Kong was always a great place to play at being a photographer. And there were some yum cha palaces and a couple of Chiu Chow restaurants that had been missing my presence for way too long.

'Get the assignment briefing sheet and your ticket and flight details from Julie,' Gordon continued, 'and try to be more careful with your gun.'

So he already knew about the incident on the tram. That was interesting. I shook my head. 'Explain to me again why regulations make me carry a gun where I'm safe and deny me one when I'm some place where people have a good reason to want me dead?'

Before he could answer I did it for him. 'I don't make the rules,' I said in a sing-song voice, 'I just carry them out. I know, I know.'

'Didn't you get my memo about that pistol?' he asked.

The Sauer was my own gun and Gordon didn't like it. It was a very compact 9mm Model 38, dating from the Second World War. My Uncle Cliff, an anti-tank gunner with the ninth division, had taken it off a dead panzer commander after El Alamein and smuggled it home as a souvenir. As a youngster I'd once tried to take it to school for show-and-tell on Anzac Day. Uncle Cliff got a bit grumpy about that. J.P. Sauer & Sohn made an attractive little pistol. The 7.62 version was even smaller than mine and very popular with Luftwaffe crews because it fitted neatly into a flight-suit pocket. I'd rediscovered the pistol in Uncle Cliff's personal stuff the week after his funeral and had our armourers rebuild it for me. I don't think Gordon was too comfortable with the Afrika Corps palm-tree-and-swastika motif neatly engraved on the pistol's grip.

I also knew he couldn't let me out the door without asking me about his access code.

'Before you go, about the password . . . '

I just loved it. Mahler, God help us. Gordon had Mahler playing on his sound system, a Mahler screensaver and a framed Mahler concert poster hanging on the office wall. He'd even tried to heavy the building manager into having Mahler muzak in the elevators. For all I knew he was wearing Mahler boxer shorts, but then I really didn't want to know.

'My fourteen-year-old niece got a new PC for her birthday. I got her to hack into the Agency's main data bank. Our security firewall is really very good. It took her five tries to get access.'

He stood at his desk, all the colour draining out of his face. I closed the door behind me, counted to three and stuck my head back in the room. 'I was only kidding about my niece breaking in with a PC,' I said.

The relief washed over him in a wave. His faith in our impregnable computer system was restored.

'It was an iMac!'

FIVE

I watched out the window as the Tullamarine airport runway dropped away beneath us. The roar of jet engines, the solid thump of the undercarriage locking up into the fuselage and the knowledge that my camera cases were stowed safely in the hold always brings back memories of my first solo assignment for D-E-D.

It was to Afghanistan in the early eighties to check out how the Mujaheddin resistance against the invading Soviet forces was going. There were rumours that they were using CIA-supplied Stinger SAMs – surface-to-air missiles – against the new Russian assault helicopters. The Poms, anxious to sell their own Blowpipe SAMs to the Mujaheddin, asked D-E-D to put a man in on their behalf to see how effective the American Stingers were. They needed someone they could deny all knowledge of to their trusted trans-Atlantic partner should things happen to go pear-shaped, and since I was young and expendable I got the gig.

I decided to create a cover of being a wildlife photographer doing a photo story on mountain goats, and with a local guide I worked my way through the Baroghil Pass from Pakistan to Afghanistan. It was an arduous journey but within days of landing in Lahore I was spending the night in a mountaintop cave listening to a band of fierce Afghan guerillas describing the impossibility of fighting off helicopter attacks with AK-47s and outdated Russian SA-7 SAMs.

The Soviet Mi-24H Hind helicopters were a nasty piece of work and the Afghans hated and feared them. A perfect battlefield assault platform, the Hind carried 128 S-5 57mm rockets, four napalm or HE bombs and a rapid-fire cannon, as well as eight fully equipped combat troops. The D model Hind also had a heavily armoured belly and cockpit protection, making it almost immune to ground fire. The bloody thing was like a tank with a five-bladed rotor on top. Apparently it also handled a bit a like a flying tank but with all that armour protecting your arse no-one really cared.

By staying above 5000 feet, Hinds could strafe the ground in total safety since the guerillas' SA-7s couldn't reach that high. But Stingers in the hands of the Mujaheddin would make it a very different ball game.

The shoulder-fired, one-man anti-aircraft system launched an infra-red, heat-seeking missile with an effective ceiling of over 15 000 feet. Sophisticated electronic counter-measure immunity ensured that when a Stinger identified a target and was on its way at 1200 miles per hour the target was history. The only possible defence was to fly so high that accurate ground targeting of enemy forces became impossible.

An hour before dawn the guerilla leader woke me with a promise to show me something exciting, which was why I was freezing my butt off on a rocky crag when the magnificent mountain goat wandered into view. The damn thing posed heroically like it knew I was there, and with its lush mane and corkscrew horns it was just too good an image to pass up. I shot about a dozen frames using trusty old Kodachrome and a Nikon F3 with a 1000mm Reflex-Nikkor lens.

After making certain the exposures of the goat were on the money, I tilted the tripod head down slightly and started shooting a series of pictures that I knew was certain to stir up a lot of interest. A convoy of battered Afghan trucks were making a run for the shelter of a canyon when a Russian Hind D appeared in the distance. The trucks scattered and when a guerilla appeared on a ledge just below me carrying a Stinger I realised it was an ambush. The Mujaheddin fighter aimed through the open sights on the launcher and when the guidance system locked onto the heat of the helicopter's twin Isotov TV-3-117 turbine engines, he pressed the trigger. The Stinger rocketed out of the launcher, and seconds later it blasted the helicopter out of the sky in a ball of flames.

When the CIA found out about my photographs they did a high-level deal with D-E-D that gave them the pictures and got me a two-year posting to Washington to do an accelerated degree in photojournalism by day and some interesting night classes in the black arts. One of my college professors saw the mountain goat pictures in my portfolio, along with some other wildlife shots, and persuaded me to submit the images to a major geographic magazine, which immediately snapped them up.

Though taken to disguise my real mission in Afghanistan, the pictures were good enough to make the cover and run inside as a full-colour ten-page spread. A very large cheque and an international reputation as a photographer came along with publication. When I returned home I pitched an idea to the director of D-E-D – set up a real live working international photographic agency as cover for D-E-D operatives.

There were the usual endless high-level meetings and finally, when all the bureaucrats involved agreed it was a good idea, WORLDPIX was born. They hired me as a photographer with great public fanfare and privately demanded I hand over all monies received from the mountain goat series. A token commission was returned to me with many thanks and WORLDPIX was on its way.

It was a raging success right from the start. Instead of trying to smuggle tiny cameras across hostile borders, our blokes just rolled up to Customs and Immigration with WORLDPIX INTERNATIONAL press passes and cameras, lenses, tripods and electronic gear coming out of their ears. We walked and talked and snapped and drank and caroused and wore vests with lots of pockets just like all the real photographers, which we actually were. And all the gregarious carrying-on that war photographers since Robert Capa have been famous for was perfect cover for information gathering.

Along with their training in espionage, D-E-D recruits had to learn to be great photographers so they could justify their place on the WORLDPIX books alongside the genuine snappers. It was hard to say if our blokes were spies who were photographers or photographers who were spies.

The whole thing was a romp until Glasnost, which turned it into a cakewalk. The Yanks were pissed off at not thinking of it first and tried to copy our set-up. But a word in the ear of some top US publishing execs had killed that. The Americans had been very touchy about misusing the freedom of the press back then. After September 11, of course, all bets were off.

The commercial success of the legitimate photographic side of our operation had been bugging me recently. With so much money coming in, the bureaucrats had become much more interested in running WORLDPIX and D-E-D as a sort of cash cow rather than an actual intelligence-gathering service, and the fun was going right out of the business.

Plus we were on the outer over the whole Iraq fiasco. The goverment hadn't been too happy with a lot of the information we'd given them. It was frequently way too accurate for their purposes and since most of our work is image-based it's a bit harder to creatively misinterpret than written data. You have to try really, really hard.

The 767 was two hours out of Melbourne when grim-faced cabin attendants started snatching half-eaten airline breakfasts back from the passengers. Lucky for me I'm a quick eater. Or perhaps not, given that the flavour-free chicken sausage was apparently taking exception to cohabiting with the scrambled egg-like something and the lukewarm brownish coffee-equivalent liquid in my stomach.

I'd started reading the complimentary morning newspaper to try to distract myself from the untoward abdominal gurgling. Since it was a Melbourne paper, football naturally dominated the front page and the lead story was a doozey. Apparently the authorities were considering banning the traditional practice of scattering the cremated remains of loyal club members on their football team's sacred home turf. A few weeks earlier a rather nasty strain of Asian flu had cut a lethal swathe through the elderly residents of several nursing homes, including many dedicated football followers, and on Saturday afternoon, following a long spell of unseasonably dry weather, a gale at the aptly nicknamed 'Windy Hill' football ground had produced a whirling dust and ash cloud of recently deceased past members so dense that an Essendon/Richmond pre-season grudge match had to be called off due to zero visibility.

As I was trying to visualise this scenario the newspaper was snatched from my grasp and I was tersely instructed to stow my tray table and return my seatback to the upright position. You could see people looking at each other and wondering if now might be a good moment to have a squiz at that safety card in the seat pocket in front of them. Moments later the pilot came on the intercom to announce he was going to make a special announcement. The elderly woman in the seat next to me crossed herself and folded her hands. The pilot paused for a while in that funny way they all seem to do, allowing us to imagine the worst possible scenario, and then when he was confident that the whole plane had a white-knuckle grip on the armrests, made his announcement in a frosty voice. They were obviously not too happy up on the flight deck.

'Ladies and gentlemen, there is no cause for alarm.' Most people would agree this is a most alarming thing to hear over any aircraft intercom. 'As you were aware, Flight 372 is scheduled as a non-stop flight to Hong Kong,' he continued, 'however, we are currently dumping fuel as we have been instructed to divert to Sydney immediately to remove one of our passengers from the aircraft. This is at the request of the Federal Police who apparently need to speak urgently to the gentleman in question. Allowing time to refuel and to remove this person's luggage from the hold, as per airline safety regulations, we estimate a minimum six-hour delay in arriving at our destination. Thank you for your attention.'

Everyone on the plane was looking warily at everyone else. It must have been pretty heavy if the feds were willing to pull back an international flight. The woman next to me began putting some very intense work into a string of rosary beads. I didn't bother to join in the general rubbernecking.

I'd already given my fellow passengers a serious once-over in the departure lounge before we boarded, after we'd all put our shoes back on and I'd turned my mobile phone off. There didn't appear to be anyone in this crowd who looked any more suspicious than usual. D-E-D gets all the travel advisories but I'm a nervous flier at the best of times and I like to keep an eye on who I'm travelling with. Like most people these days, I find the joys of international jet travel long gone.

Was there a sky cop on this flight? An innocent-looking passenger armed with a compact Model 26 Glock getting himself ready to shoot 9mm high-impact frangible bullets into anyone making a suspicious move towards the front of the plane? Thank God my stomach had finally settled down. Right now wasn't really the time to have to make an urgent dash to one of the lavatories up the aisle just behind business class.

A gaggle of cabin crew had gone into a tight huddle near the galley and a couple of them seemed to be looking my way. The purser left the group and took a suit bag from one of the lockers. There was something uncomfortably familiar about the bag. The purser walked down the aisle and dropped it in my lap. He wasn't smiling.

'You'll need your coat,' he said. 'It's still a bit chilly in Sydney.'

By the time the 767 dropped its landing gear and the nose tilted for the descent into Kingsford Smith our major danger was that the rosary beads racing through the fingers of the woman next to me would burst into flames. All the other passengers were sitting up straight, looking directly ahead and keeping their thoughts to themselves. I didn't know about the weather in Sydney but the atmosphere was pretty bloody frosty on board the plane at that moment.

A mobile staircase and some federal and state police cars were waiting at the Botany Bay end of the runway when the 767 pulled up with its tyres smoking. We'd made one of those fast and hard landings, the sort you can usually blame on a nervous copilot or a captain in a bit of a bad mood. I guessed our pilot might have had a hot date lined up in Honkers. The silence onboard the aircraft was deafening as I made my way down the aisle to the starboard door. I offered the grim-faced purser my bottle of duty-free whisky, a mumbled apology and my baggage claim stubs so they could find my gear in the cargo hold. Two hundred pairs of very angry eyes bored into my back and the pilot didn't open the cockpit door to thank me for choosing to fly on an airline that I was pretty damned sure would never want to see me again. What was I going to do with all those frequent-flyer points?

I fled down the stairs to where Tas Johnson from the Sydney office was waiting beside an unmarked red police Commodore with one of those blue flashing magnetic cop bubbles stuck on the roof. A highway patrol pursuit car fitted with all the bells and whistles was parked next to it, engine burbling. Obviously a lead car for a very quick trip to wherever we were headed. This was some kind of reception committee and Tas was looking grim.

'Harry's down,' was all he said. It was enough.

'Hard?' I asked, but I think I already knew the answer.

Tas nodded. 'Real hard. Coffee shop in Double Bay. They're giving us every green light to the city.'

As we roared out onto the freeway with lights and sirens we passed two airport fire engines heading into the international terminal's short-term car park. They had lights and sirens going too and I could see flames and smoke billowing up from the centre of the car park. Somebody else was obviously having a bad day.

SIX

Double Bay is a leafy, high-tone suburb with top-end dress shops, mid-range patisseries and camp hairdressers so over the top they'd make Liberace look like a wharfie. The Bay is one of those places where very stylish women double-park very expensive cars on the way to sip very expensive coffee in surprisingly ordinary cafés. Outside the Vienna Café, Knox Street was jammed with police cars. Uniformed officers were holding back a mob of gawkers and TV news vans were rigging their microwave dishes for direct links to the eleven o'clock news. The Vienna sprawls out of an arcade and onto the footpath. Usually neat and tidy, it was a mess of overturned tables and broken dishes. And blood. Lots and lots of blood.

Harry was on his back, against a shattered mirrored wall, a coffee cup still in his fingers, chunks of croissant spread over his chest and what was left of his face. Uniformed police were taking statements from waiters and customers, most of whom appeared to be in shock. I knew the plain clothes homicide cop who was bending over the other two bodies. I didn't have to ask. One was Jimmy Stannopolous, who ran most of the drugs and girls in Sydney, and the other was Albert Wilson Stannard, a prominent racing identity, which is how the New South Wales libel laws make investigative reporters describe high-profile people with no visible means of support and way too much money.

'Sorry,' the cop said, 'looks like a hit and your mate got caught in the middle. Wrong place, wrong time.'

A bod from forensics was dusting cups for prints at a table near the entrance. I looked at the saucer. The bill had been paid. I sat down, suddenly not feeling so good. Last time Harry and I had breakfast together I pointed out how many grams of fat there were in a croissant. Told him they were deadly. Might even have said they'd be the death of him one day.

At spy school they teach you that proficient agents, aiming to maintain a low profile, try to avoid appearing on the eleven o'clock morning news throwing up in the gutter, so I took a lot of deep breaths.

'Okay, tell me what you know so far,' I said, when I felt confident about keeping my airline breakfast down.

Peter Sturdee, the cop, looked at his notebook. 'These two yobs,' he said, indicating Stannopolous and Stannard, 'have coffee here at ten most days. Life of the idle rich, eh?'

He flipped to the next page of his notebook. 'Always the same table,' he went on, 'number eight. The hit man comes in at about nine-thirty, average height, average weight, average looks. Very expensive suit. Average briefcase. Orders a pot of tea, Darjeeling, no milk, no discernible accent, and proceeds to read the *Herald*.'

I nodded.

'The garbage here,' he said, indicating the dead mobsters, 'show up just after ten. Harry comes in at around ten-fifteen and about five minutes later our mysterious Mr Average pays his bill, folds his newspaper, takes a machine pistol out of his briefcase and blows away table eight.'

He looked at me. 'Harry was unlucky enough to be sitting at the table behind them. Collateral damage, as the Yanks like to say.'

For a moment I considered clocking him. That 'collateral damage' was one of my mates. I let it pass but I guess Sturdee saw the look in my eye.

'Ah, sorry,' he said, 'that didn't come out right.'

We stared at each other and then his eyes went back to his notebook. 'The hit man puts his gun and newspaper in the case and walks out to a white Laser parked at the kerb and drives away. No-one gets the rego number, of course. Probably a rental anyway.'

I looked at the floor of the restaurant amongst the broken china, food scraps and blood – no shell cases.

'So we're talking about a simple underworld hit?' I said. 'And Harry blunders into the middle? That's very neat.'

Sturdee was looking defensive. Maybe he thought I was

getting aggro because of my friend. Maybe I was. Harry and I had trained on the island together. We weren't exactly bosom buddies but we went way back. And in our business that counts for a lot.

'Look,' the cop said, 'I know you've got a personal involvement here but this is my job. We get gangland hits like this every once in a while.'

I stood up. Sturdee was an okay bloke for a walloper. We'd always both pretended I really was just a photographer even though he probably had some kind of idea otherwise. A few drinks together in the past and the odd pie floater at *Harry's Café de Wheels* meant we were sort of mates, but right now I had a lot of anger to get out.

'No,' I snapped, 'you never fucking get hits like this. You get five pounds of sweating out-of-date gelignite under a car seat, wired to the ignition, or an icepick in the skull down some dark alley, or a junkie with a sawn-off shotgun paid off in heroin or with a nasty little hot shot if they want him to keep his trap shut permanently.'

The news crews were getting interested in the man yelling at the cop in the shot-up café so I took a deep breath and managed to calm myself.

'Your average gangland hit around here is by a bumbling amateur or a bumbling semi-pro,' I said quietly. 'Our shooter sat in a busy restaurant for forty-five minutes without attracting any undue attention. He paid his bill, left a five-dollar tip and used a brass catcher on his weapon, so forensics don't even have any shell casings to work on. He was cool enough to take his morning newspaper, as well as his gun, to walk quietly over to his very conveniently parked car and to drive himself away.'

I glanced towards the forensic technician.

'I doubt if Sherlock over there will even find any fingerprints worth having. Not from this guy.'

Sturdee looked at me and wisely decided to keep his mouth shut.

'No, mate,' I said, 'this was a very big and very expensive hit. Bigger than these two arseholes had any right to expect.'

A female constable came over and whispered in Sturdee's ear. They walked across to one of the police Commodores where he used the radio. I think he was glad to get away from me, which was okay. He probably didn't like my version of events since it wouldn't allow him to tie things up quite so neatly. As he walked back I knew what he was going to say. Okay, if this guy was such a pro, he'd ask, how come he could only manage five slugs into each of the two hoodlums? He completely missed with the other twenty. Which was true. The missing twenty rounds had all gone squarely into my mate Harry.

'The shooter's car turned up at the airport,' Sturdee said. 'In the short-term car park. On fire.'

Well, that explained the two fire engines I'd seen. It wasn't hard to guess what they'd find once the shell of the car cooled down. This guy was a total pro. Stick a thermite pencil down the barrel and leave the gun in the boot sitting over the fuel tank. The white heat of the thermite melts the weapon beyond all possibility of identification and then the molten steel burns through to the fuel tank. The exploding car causes enough distraction that no-one would ever remember exactly what flight a very average-looking bloke had taken out of the country. Right about now he'd be sitting comfortably at ten thousand metres somewhere finishing off his paper and sipping on the complimentary orange juice, mixed with expensive champagne if he was up the pointy end.

Sturdee was still looking at his feet so I knew there was something more.

'It's been quite exciting out at the airport this morning,' he said. 'They pulled some luggage off a flight to Hong Kong that was diverted to our fair city earlier today. The driver stopped the trolley halfway back to baggage claim to take a leak behind an aerobridge. Not too hygienic but the bugger's bladder probably saved his life. He was walking back towards the trolley when his load blew up.'

Sturdee stared at me. 'They reckon he's going to make it, but apparently chunks of Nikon cameras are still falling all over the tarmac.'

SEVEN

Why Harry had been hit was a mystery and I needed time on my own to think it through. I took a taxi to Bondi Beach and had the driver drop me on Campbell Parade near the pavilion. For a minute I considered stopping by my flat in Luxor Mansions but decided against it.

The name Luxor Mansions might conjure up visions of an Egyptian palace overlooking the Nile but the old Luxor was more of a thirties copy of an English seaside hotel overlooking the beach. My apartment was on the top floor with views from the seawater pool at the Icebergs swimming club right round to the rocks at Ben Buckler point. The vacuuming and dusting were long overdue and I really couldn't face another depressing scene this morning.

I thought I saw a brief flash of a face behind my living-room curtains, which made me smile. At least my house plants should still be alive. My elderly widowed neighbour

Mrs Templeton watered them every few days when I was away. She also collected my mail and popped the odd shepherd's pie into my freezer for when I needed a bit of comfort food. Mrs T made a great shepherd's pie. In return I sometimes walked her dog Dougal, an ugly wheezing pug with a face like the front end of a Datsun 120Y that had hit a brick wall at high speed.

Mrs Templeton had lived in the Mansions since she arrived from Scotland in the early fifties with her husband, a marine engineer. I'd never met the man but from the tales she told her late husband obviously had some moxie since he'd survived having three ships torpedoed out from under him on the North Atlantic convoy runs during the war. I'd have packed seafaring in as a career after the first dunking. The waters of the North Atlantic are bloody freezing, even in summer, and to top things off he couldn't swim. However, he apparently had treading water down to a fine art, and that had saved his life, even on the occasion when, in the panic of abandoning a burning ship at night, he'd grabbed his new Harris Tweed sports coat from behind the cabin door instead of the life jacket. When hauled out of the water by the Royal Navy two hours later he was almost blue with hypothermia but beautifully dressed.

Mrs T and I would often drink tea and chat in her sunroom while Dougal grunted and snuffled under my feet like a small black asthmatic vacuum cleaner, sucking up the crumbs of her delicious homemade shortbread biscuits. Mostly she'd reminisce about Scotland and complain about our landlord, who was actually me since I'd bought the whole building in the late eighties when the cool people couldn't understand why anybody would want to live at the beach amongst the bikies and junkies. I kept my ownership quiet, of course, and ignored the managing agent when he told me I could turf Mrs Templeton out and quadruple the rent. I didn't need the money and those regular cuppas with Mrs T and the mutt were a welcome dose of reality.

From the Parade I walked down the path past the old Russian regulars playing dominoes in the sun behind the thirties beachside pavilion and then out along the promenade towards my favourite coffee joint on the beach. It was late morning, so the disgustingly fit personal trainers and their deranged victims were long gone from the exercise area in the park. Just a handful of dedicated local sunbakers were sprawled on the sand and even the seagulls seemed to be taking it easy. The only real activity was a bunch of tykes from the surfing school paddling their boards out into some baby waves.

Soggy Togs is a neatly fitted out little café in a huddle of shops located opposite the north end of the beach. Moderately comfortable seats, an excellent breakfast, great coffee and a fantastic view. It was still too early for lunch and the café was empty except for a couple of out-of-work actors reading Brecht. The tables at the front give you a panoramic view of the sweep of the beach right across to the Icebergs and the start of the spectacular walking path round the cliff tops to Tamarama and Bronte. The back tables are out of line of sight with the doorway, however, so I took one of those and ordered a latte.

I contemplated having a piece of cheesecake as a sort of tribute to Harry but decided against it. Harry only ever ate cheesecake from Medy's on Glenayre Avenue. Someone had once told him it was 99 per cent fat-free and that Medy's were the official cheesecake suppliers to the Clovelly Bowling Club. Harry had always maintained that when it came to cheesecake those Clovelly lawn bowlers really knew their onions.

I sipped my coffee and tried to sort things out but none of this morning's events made any sense. Harry dead in an apparent gangland shooting that seemed way too well organised, and my luggage exploding only moments after coming out of the hold of a 767 that should have been cruising at ten thousand metres en route to Hong Kong. Every damned thing in those camera cases had been checked three times. Once to make sure all the cameras and lenses were working and complete; the second time for anything that might suggest I was more than just a working photographer; and thirdly, for anything nasty. And Graeme Rutherford wasn't one for making mistakes. Plus there were the regular security checks at the airport. Had to be clean as a whistle every time or they wouldn't reach the cargo hold.

I finished my coffee and went out the back door for a piss in the cramped dunny up the outside stairs. While I was washing my hands I remembered my mobile was still switched off.

I turned it back on and as I was waving my hands under the bloody useless hot-air drier it beeped. There was a text message from Harry, reading '*See you there*'. I checked the Time Sent display: 7:10 this morning, just as I was boarding my flight. A shiver went up my spine.

When I sat back down at my table, Alex, the café's owner, handed me a second cup of coffee and a plain white envelope. 'This is for you, I guess,' he said. 'Someone must have left it on the counter while I was out in the kitchen.'

The envelope was hand-addressed and directed, very succinctly, to 'the man in the back corner'. When people are getting shot and your luggage is blowing up, any unidentified package anonymously delivered becomes a definite worry. This one had a thin, hard rectangular centre.

I held the envelope up to the light but all I could see was the outline of what looked like an audio cassette tape. There was no sign of any wires or other nasties. I shook the envelope gently and whatever was inside rattled like an audio cassette tape. I decided there was nothing to indicate it was a bomb, but to be on the safe side I carefully slit the bottom edge of the envelope with a knife and checked the contents. It *was* an audio cassette tape.

The tape was unmarked and unremarkable. Luckily the café's sound system was a CD/radio/cassette combo. One of the out–of–work actors gave me a dirty look when I stopped the Norah Jones CD mid-song and inserted the cassette into the player. Bugger 'em, I thought. Anyway, I preferred Tierney

Sutton. For my money, she's got a wider range and better diction.

I hit the 'Play' button. It chilled me to hear the voice.

'*Hi, this is Harry. I'm out – you know what to do.*'

There were a couple of messages from women who would never have their calls returned and apparently BlockBuster Video at the Junction really and truly wanted their DVD of *Zulu* back. It was the fourth message that froze my blood.

'*Meet me at the Vienna in the Bay around ten tomorrow morning. The table's booked in your name. It's important.*'

It was my voice, no question about it, but it was a call I'd never made. I really didn't have time to even try to figure this one out as the first bullet came through the open window and struck the player. The cassette ejected neatly and I grabbed it as a second bullet ploughed through the coffee cups stacked on top of the espresso machine. No big bangs audible so the weapon was obviously silenced. The two actors were looking shocked and I hoped they were soaking it all up as a sense memory they could use at their next audition. As for me, I decided it was time to exit Soggy Togs speedily, stage left.

I went out the rear door and sprinted up the concrete stairs that led past the toilet and back to Campbell Parade. There was a squeal of tyres behind me on the promenade and the roar of an engine pushing full revs. I was racing for the top, hoping to beat them to the roadway, but it wasn't to be. A little man with a very big gun was already waiting for me on the corner. He smiled, apparently pleased to see me and probably very happy that it was going to be such an easy shot. Since I'd had to clear security at the airport my Sauer 9mm was safely locked up in the armoury back in Melbourne. These days you couldn't talk your way through anything at an airport.

I knew I wouldn't be able get to him before he pulled the trigger but he coughed suddenly and seemed to jump sideways at the same time. The pistol dropped from his hand as he slammed hard against the wooden fence. There was a confused look on his face and a dark stain marked the palings as he slid slowly to the ground, slumping in a limp heap.

'Move it or lose it!' a voice yelled.

As I sprinted towards the red Ford Mustang with its open passenger door, I bent to scoop up the shooter's fallen pistol. Before I'd fully closed the door the big V8 engine had us hurtling down the Parade and heading towards the city up Bondi Road. I looked over at my chauffeur. She was driving very fast and very confidently and watching all the mirrors carefully.

'Nice wheels,' I said.

She nodded. ''67 GT/A, with the Holley carbs. Not crazy about the steering wheel being on this side though.'

The seat I was sitting in seemed strangely uncomfortable. Reaching down, my hand found a silenced Browning Hi Power semi-automatic. The pistol was warm. 'When I saw you on that tram, I reckoned you knew how to handle a gun,' I said.

Her slate-grey eyes flicked off the mirror with the hint of a smile. Of course. Sniper's eyes. No wonder she could bloody shoot.

EIGHT

We left the Mustang in the basement of the David Jones underground parking lot at Bondi Junction and took the escalators up to the store. The DJs food hall was surprisingly quiet and for once I could have grabbed a seat at the fresh seafood bar without having to fight for it. It used to be a real jungle in there but they'd installed numbered ticket dispensers in the deli a few years back, more for customer safety than for convenience. The system had certainly cut down on the injuries when you tried to pick up some corned beef or kassler or pastrami; the elbows on some of those elderly eastern suburbs matrons can be bloody lethal.

Today though, the champagne and those plump and succulent Sydney Rock oysters on ice had very limited appeal. When people have spent the entire morning trying to kill you, you tend to focus on other things. At the top of the escalators we split up. In the menswear department I grabbed a lightweight reversible jacket and a white wide-brimmed bowler's hat. I paid cash and my change came with a pitying look from the young sales assistant when I said I'd be wearing the clothes out.

Grey Eyes was already waiting for me at the Grafton Street exit. Good-looking, a dead shot and a very fast shopper; my idea of the perfect woman. She was wearing an ugly green coat and a baseball cap which lessened the perfect woman image a tad but she obviously knew exactly what to do in a situation like this without being told. That can be attractive too. Her briefcase was stuffed inside a cheap yellow daypack slung over her left shoulder.

We crossed the road to the bus interchange, walked briskly down the stairs to the underground railway station, bought tickets to Chatswood from the machine and smiled for the closed circuit security cameras above the turnstiles. At the bottom of the escalators we walked straight onto a waiting train. A friendly female voice over the station's loudspeakers announced the train was heading for the city and points south.

Edgecliff is the first stop on the Eastern Suburbs line and by the time our train got there I'd reversed my jacket to the dark blue side and dropped the bowler's hat next to a sleeping drunk. The woman pulled a plastic DJs shopping bag from the daypack and slipped her briefcase into it. Her silenced Browning was inside but I'd wiped my prints off the hit man's weapon and tucked it under the front seat of the

Mustang back in the shopping-centre car park. She stuffed the green coat into the empty daypack and left it next to the drunk. Lucky bloke, when he woke up he'd have a whole new wardrobe just in time for winter.

As the train stopped the woman reversed her baseball cap and put on a pair of aviator-style sunglasses. I'm not a fan of the back-to-front baseball cap but she made it work. We exited the carriage through separate doors and stayed well clear of each other on the escalator and at the turnstiles. When we reached the road I watched as she took her briefcase from the shopping bag, which she then carefully folded and placed in a council rubbish bin. This girl was most definitely a pro. I didn't even know her name yet, but we were already working like a well-oiled machine.

It was one of those beautiful sunny Sydney autumn days as we headed down New South Head Road, walking in the general direction of the city. As we passed the Rushcutters Bay marina on our right I guided her left into Neild Avenue and up past the back of the old White City Tennis Courts.

'You have a plan?' she asked.

'You like Italian food?'

She nodded. 'I love pizza.'

I shook my head. Jesus, what the hell were they teaching them at spy school these days?

We walked past some new-car dealerships and a number of warehouses that had been recently converted into loft apartments. The building on the corner of the next lane stuck out like a sore thumb. Well, perhaps not so much a sore thumb as a very elegant and well-manicured index finger. It was a two-storey Tuscan-style villa with shuttered windows and Juliet balconies upstairs. I stopped.

She looked at the sign.

'Buon Ricordo. This is your plan?' she asked. 'A restaurant?'

I nodded. 'Step One: Never proceed to Step Two on an empty stomach.'

She pushed against the heavy front door. It was locked.

'Plan B?'

'This way.' We walked up the laneway, in through an unlocked tall steel gate, across the small courtyard, and into the kitchen. Armando was yelling at an apprentice in Italian-accented English or Australian-accented Italian. The apprentice might possibly have been listening in Thai but it was obvious he was getting the message. Armando smiled when he saw me and then stopped smiling when he saw my face.

'Upstairs is empty,' he said. 'Phillip is just finishing setting up for dinner.'

I led the woman towards the stairs.

'You and your friend are hungry?' Armando asked. Even after thirty years in Australia he was still so Italian. Trouble always equals food. Got a problem, get a plate. Got a big problem, it's that-a-way to the table with the antipasto.

'She loves pizza, and I'm a bit peckish.'

The woman held out her hand to Armando.

'I'm Grace,' she said.

He took her hand in both of his and beamed at her. Being Neapolitan and in the restaurant trade since you were fourteen really teaches you how to smile at the ladies. Even pushing sixty, Armando still had it. Bastard.

'I'm Armando, bella,' he said. 'For such a beautiful signorina I think we can do a lot better than pizza.'

He was so damned Italian. But at least now we both knew her name.

NINE

We made our way through an elegant dining room that wouldn't have been out of place in Florence or Venice.

'Thanks for the pizza comment,' Grace said. 'Now he thinks I'm a real yokel.'

'He's Italian and he's from Naples,' I said. 'He thinks everyone's a yokel. He can't help it. It's genetic.'

At the top of the stairs was another elegant dining room, filled with paintings and sculptures and flooded with late-morning sun. Phillip, Armando's head waiter, looked up from the table he was setting and smiled. Phillip is an excellent waiter, experienced, discreet and with a flint-dry wit thrown in. I'd been at the next table one evening while he was carefully deboning a whole snapper for some whiz-bang real-estate developer and his latest poppet. The property mogul was obviously feeling good about his life as he pushed back his chair and looked happily around the busy dining room.

'Well Phillip,' he said, 'I wonder what the poor people are doing tonight, eh?'

Without missing a beat and in a low but perfectly pitched voice Phillip answered, 'They're filleting your fish for you, sir.'

I'd almost choked on my glass of Amarone.

Gemma, Armando's wife, came out of the office and kissed me on both cheeks.

'You in trouble?' she asked.

I nodded. I liked restaurant people. The good ones can suss out a situation in nothing flat and they also know when to keep mum.

'You're having lunch?' she asked, but it wasn't really a question. She turned to Grace, held her gaze for a moment and then smiled, put out her hand and introduced herself. That was a good sign. I trusted Gemma's intuition. Sure, Grey Eyes here had saved my bacon earlier, but it never hurts to get a second opinion.

Gemma removed two place settings from a table set for four and we sat down. Grace put her briefcase on one of the spare chairs and popped the latches. I noticed we'd both picked chairs that faced the stairs. Phillip brought some olive oil and rolls and grissini and filled our water glasses. He asked if we wanted something from the bar but I said we'd just have wine with whatever Armando decided we should eat for lunch. Grace agreed. I think she was warming to my plan.

Gemma went back to her office and Phillip headed

downstairs. I realised that I could relax and suddenly I felt a thousand years old.

'So who wants you dead, and why?' Grace asked.

She was very tanned, even for someone with grey eyes and raven hair. The skin colour, plus the high cheekbones and shape of her eyes, hinted at Native American blood somewhere in her ancestry.

I shrugged. I wasn't going to tell her. Besides that, I had no idea. And anyway we hadn't been formally introduced.

'My name's Alby,' I said, 'Alby Murdoch. I'm a freelance photographer.'

I put out my hand and she shook it. Firmly, the way Americans do, believing it makes them look honest, steadfast and true. Trouble is I've met a lot of real arseholes with firm handshakes.

'Grace Goodluck,' she said, smiling. It was one of those don't-mess-with-me smiles, intended to remind you she had a loaded nine mil within easy reach.

'What are you working on, Mr Murdoch?' she asked.

'I was going to Hong Kong to do a picture story on the Dragon Boat Races,' I said.

She let that answer hang there for a long moment, then shook her head and smiled that smile again. She reached into her briefcase and handed me a thick file. A quick skim of the contents took me ten minutes. It was a marvel of detail. Very impressive. Far more comprehensive than my file in Gordon's office, the one in the triple-locked filing cabinet that I wasn't supposed to have access to.

'Did we miss anything?' she asked.

I shook my head. 'Not really,' I said. 'I actually had the clap twice in 1982 and it was the left knee that got damaged in that punch-up in Bangkok. Otherwise it's pretty accurate.'

The Bangkok stoush had become legendary in certain circles. It was my first overseas assignment for D-E-D and I was young and impetuous and pissed as a cricket when I tried to save the Swedish reporter's honour in a bar full of boozed-up Aussie newspaper correspondents.

The glory days of Vietnam and Cambodia were long gone by then and a lot of formerly high-flying reporters were having to cover stories like a half-hearted army coup against the ruling generals in the Thai capital and they weren't very happy about it. They were spoiling for some fun or some action and of course the Swedish reporter really should have known better than to walk into a joint like that at that time of night wearing a tight T-shirt with the word 'PRESS' emblazoned invitingly across her ample chest.

The only thing that stopped me from being beaten to a pulp was the welcome intervention of an Aussie ex-special forces type who was quietly drinking in the bar with a Vietnamese bloke. The two of them dragged me out from under the scrum and dumped me outside in the street.

When I passed the file back Grace handed me another. Hers now. Much more impressive than mine, even with the shorter time frame. Grace Goodluck, born December 1971. West Point early 90s, First Captain senior class, which meant she was better than all the men, no small feat. Military Police, Military Intelligence, G2 and G4, then secondment to the US Department of Justice as Liaison. Combat Infantry Badge – so she'd mixed it up where the bullets were flying – and a specialist rating as Marksman. Currently she was ranked captain. With a record like that she couldn't be far off a bump-up to major. Her maternal grandfather was the one with the Navaho blood.

It was an impressive file. Someone with a suspicious mind might say almost too good to be true. But in my line of work all the good cover stories are built on a spine of truth. So even if only a quarter of what was in this file was true the woman definitely had the goods in some areas. I handed the folder back to her. The reality was she'd saved my life, so I decided to risk trusting her. There also didn't seem to be anybody else around I could rely on. And she *was* a Sagittarian, if you chose to believe that part of her file.

'Okay,' I said, 'as far as I know I'm not working on anything hot.' This was true.

'What about Harry Wardell?' she asked. 'And by the way, I'm sorry about how that came down.'

'Thanks,' I said. 'All Harry and I had on was a routine vetting of US personnel at Bitter Springs. It was a dog of an assignment, just a make-work deal, and Harry offered to do it all himself to pay back a favour. And exactly why does the US Department of Justice want to know, anyway?'

'I'm running an investigation into some irregularities

with the AMC and Harry's name came up in the course of my inquiries.'

The Air Mobility Command is a sort of gigantic in-house United Airlines for the American armed forces, flying troops and supplies all over the world. How the hell would Harry be mixed up with that? And there was something about the way she used the word 'irregularities'.

'So when Harry's name came up you linked him to me?'

She nodded.

'You free to tell me about these irregularities?' I asked.

She smiled. 'Seems like someone has misplaced three of our Globemasters.'

I took a sip of my water while I considered this. The four-engined C-17 Globemaster military transport was a bloody big plane, with the ability to lift almost any piece of US Army mobile hardware. They could carry the M1 Abrams main battle tank, up to four UH-60 Blackhawk transport helicopters, or even a couple of the AH-64 Apache attack helicopters. While not as big as the C-5 Galaxy, the C-17 weighed over a hundred tons empty and was just under fifty-five metres long, so you'd certainly know about it if someone parked one on your foot or across your driveway. Maybe you could lose one – but not three. That was getting way beyond careless.

'So you've checked down the back of the couch?'

'Yep, a handful of quarters, a couple of nickels and a half-eaten Oreo. But no Globemasters.' She got up. 'Where's the bathroom?'

'Bottom of the stairs,' I said, 'on the left as we came up. Yours is the topless woman.'

The toilet doors were decorated with paintings by the local artist Kerrie Lester, and she'd certainly approached the commission with a sense of humour. On the Ladies', a life-size, bare-breasted woman in a swirling skirt had protruding red nipples screwed onto her voluptuous bosom, and the bloke painted on the Men's door wore ballet slippers and nothing else. You could catch a glimpse of his pale pink penis from half the tables in the main dining room. Quite surprisingly, the effect was rather charming.

While she was gone I checked my mobile phone. Nothing. I knew I should call the office but something told me to just lie low for a bit longer.

Heavy-duty hit men, a bomb in my camera case and now this woman was looking for three missing military transport planes. How the hell could Harry and I turn up in the middle of an investigation into something like that?

I really had to get my head around what was happening here and when they run hypothetical scenarios like this at spy school the first thing the instructors try to drum into you is 'TRUST NO-ONE!'. What I needed to do as quickly as possible was to put some distance between me and the people who had me marked for an early and very permanent retirement. At least I was pretty sure she wasn't one of them. Of course, the second thing the instructors try to make clear is that 'pretty sure' can sometimes get you pretty dead.

When Grace came back up she was carrying a mobile phone and she looked distracted. I don't think it was just the toilet doors.

'You okay?'

'I think Step Two is to get out of town – fast,' she said. She took a second phone from her briefcase, swapped SIM cards and made sure both handsets were switched off. Carrying a mobile phone in 'on' mode is like wearing a flashing light on your head, waving a flag and shouting, *Here I am, come and get me!*

'After this morning's events I need to find somewhere safe to sort things out and I think you do too.'

'Great minds think alike,' I said.

'Ours too.'

I liked that. A wry sense of humour isn't something you find every day in the folks at the US Department of Justice. And especially not in someone who looked like they might have just had a disturbing phone conversation.

'Armando has a property a couple of hours out of town,' I suggested. 'It's off the beaten track and he's got a few thousand olive trees we can hide behind.'

She shook her head. 'I was thinking of putting a little more distance between us and them. Got a passport handy?'

Her 'them' had a ring to it that I didn't much like. And not '*your* passport' but '*a* passport'. Captain Grace Goodluck was sounding more covert ops than Department of Justice but I really didn't seem to have any choice.

'Not on me,' I said, 'but close by.'

'I can get us on a plane out of the country,' she said.

'They'll be watching the airports.'

'Not a commercial passenger flight, a cargo freighter.'

That could work. 'I've got friends in Bali,' I said.

'I know.'

'Right.' Who the hell was she? 'Sounds like we have Step Two then.'

She swung round at a noise on the stairs. Her hand was in the briefcase but she relaxed when she saw it was just Phillip with our lunch. Armando was right behind him with a salad bowl and a bottle of wine. Step One was coming along nicely.

'I made you two plates,' he said. 'I figured you wouldn't want to share.'

He was looking at me when he said it and he was right about that. Slender ribbons of fettuccine glistened under a rich creamy sauce and the gently fried egg resting on top. Phillip put the plates on the table and then ground a generous amount of parmigiano reggiano over the eggs.

'Mmm. Pasta carbonara?' Grace said.

Armando looked pained but covered by making it seem like uncorking the wine needed a little extra effort. 'Carbonara is a dish from Roma,' he said. 'This is *fettuccine al tartufovo*, a speciality of the house.' He picked up a spoon and fork and broke the still-runny yolk open before mixing the egg and parmesan gently through the creamy pasta. An exquisite aroma wafted up from the plate. 'The egg has been infused with truffle,' he explained.

'Okay, not pasta carbonara,' Grace said. 'My apologies.'

Armando smiled and poured some red wine into a glass. He tasted it and then filled two more glasses. I glanced at the label. It was a 1998 Montepulciano d'Abruzzo. Grace had already taken a mouthful of the pasta.

'Armando and Nick the sommelier have a running battle over what wine goes best with this dish,' I said.

Grace glanced up from her plate with a look of wonder in her eyes. 'Nothing could match this, Armando,' she said, 'It's stunning.'

She was right about that.

'Nick tends towards a fully oaked local chardonnay a bit on the dryish side,' I said, 'but I have to go with Armando on a light to medium-bodied Italian red.' I sipped my wine. It was very good and I was grateful for the distraction.

'You are aiming to complement the earthy flavours of the truffle,' Armando explained to Grace.

She nodded and smiled politely but the expression on her face said that right now she wasn't going to use her mouth for anything as trivial as talking.

'Ask Gemma to ring down to the kitchen if you want anything else,' Armando said.

'Probably just coffee,' I said. 'Plus that envelope Gemma's been keeping for me, and your car keys.'

Armando went to the office and came back with a thick

A4 envelope and a set of keys.

Grace had finished her fettuccine and was looking at my plate. No way known! She might have saved my life earlier but there are limits to my gratitude. I pushed the salad and the bread in her direction.

'We'll leave your car in the parking lot at the international air cargo terminal,' she said to Armando. 'The parking ticket will be in the glove compartment and we'll text you the bay number. Got a spare set of keys?'

He nodded.

'You couldn't do us a small picnic basket, could you, mate?' I asked. 'It might be a long flight.'

Armando put the car keys on the table and looked at me. 'Let's not have a repeat of what happened last time I lent you my car.'

People just don't appreciate how difficult it is to find someone to discreetly patch up a half dozen bullet holes in the door panels of a Prado. 'Hey, c'mon mate,' I said, 'it was good as new when I brought it back.'

Grace looked up at Armando, who was shaking his head.

'Maybe I should drive then,' she said, picking up the keys.

'Fine by me,' I said, picking up the wine bottle.

TEN

We made one detour on our way to the airport. Byron Oxenbould, or 'Boxer' to his friends, lived on the top floor of probably the last remaining unrenovated loft building in Surry Hills and he wasn't all that pleased to see me.

'Keep your bloody hair on!' he yelled as he unbolted the heavy steel door to his apartment in response to my pounding on the DO NOT DISTURB sign. Then, 'Oh, it's just you,' and then, 'Jesus,' when he saw Grace.

I did the introductions. 'Byron, Grace, Grace, Byron.'

'I'll put some pants on,' he said. He was naked.

'Grateful for small mercies, Boxer,' I said.

'Get rooted,' Byron snapped as he stumbled across to the curtained-off area that served as his bedroom. A pithy riposte like that really demonstrates the value of an expensive private-school education. 'I've been on night shoots for the last two weeks,' he continued from behind the curtain, 'and you're all I bloody need. What's the panic anyway?'

I walked over to the kitchen window to check the street and make sure we weren't being followed. The coffee maker was warm. Byron was the only person I knew with a four-group restaurant espresso machine in his kitchen. The coffee machine was all he had on his benchtop; there wasn't room for anything else.

The loft was a huge open warehouse space with creaking wooden floorboards, high ceilings and large windows currently covered by curtains made of theatrical blackout material. There was a living space made up of mismatched chairs and sofas he'd rescued from the streets, surrounding a giant plasma-screen TV. Benches and old wooden tables around the loft's walls were strewn with electrical equipment, soldering irons, vintage reel-to-reel tape recorders, modern Nagra recorders and assorted microphones. There were also numerous computers in various stages of disassembly or reassembly; with Byron you could never tell which.

'I need you to listen to a tape and tell me all about it,' I said.

Byron walked out of his bedroom in a blue T-shirt and jeans. The T-shirt had a graphic of a movie camera on the front and read 'Panavision Film Crew'. Byron was about thirty, and good-looking, I suppose. Women seemed to think he was, and I guess that's all that counts. He was a sound recordist on feature films and TV commercials and very good at his job. He also did the odd bit of freelance sound stealing for D-E-D from time to time, when the film business was quiet and our own surveillance guys were overloaded.

'Want coffee?' he asked, flicking the switch on the industrial-size grinder. It sounded like a 747 in reverse thrust.

I shook my head. When the noise stopped he looked at Grace. She shook her head as well. Byron fed ground coffee into the portafilter, packed it down with a stainless steel tamper I'd brought him from New York and locked the handle into the group.

He pressed a button and the pump started rumbling. A smoky-sweet aroma filled the air as the dark coffee trickled down into a small espresso cup.

Byron yawned. 'We had a five o'clock call and then the director dicked around all night and the lead actress couldn't remember her lines and the dolly grip kept stuffing up his moves. Bloody disaster. I've never been happier to see the sun come up.'

'How was the catering?' I asked.

Byron and I had met one year when I took a forced sabbatical and did stills photography on a couple of low-budget movies. Film people work hard and do long hours and the quality of the on-set catering is a major factor in crew morale, especially on night shoots.

'Spaghetti Sisters,' he grinned.

'Nice,' I said, nodding. The Spaghetti Sisters were gorgeous identical twins who did excellent meals with an Italian bent, were known for their fabulous desserts, and one or both of them had a crush on Byron. Byron had slept with both of them, or one of them twice and it drove him crazy not knowing which it was. He stirred sugar into the coffee and gulped it down.

'Where's this tape?' he asked.

I handed it over. 'It's from Harry's answering machine.'

'Jesus,' Byron said, 'he still using that old clunker? I must have fixed that thing a dozen times for him. He'll take that bloody machine with him to his grave.'

He walked over to a bench, dropped the tape into a player and pushed the hinged door closed, using a remote control to turn on the large TV at the same time. The sound on the TV was off but the image of me in the middle of the café yelling at Detective Sturdee was very clear. So was the logo of the café. My voice came out of a speaker somewhere, inviting Harry to meet me at the Vienna and take twenty soft-nosed slugs in the chest and face.

Byron stared at me. 'What's going on?'

'Someone shot Harry in the café after I invited him out for breakfast.'

'Jesus.'

'Only thing is, I didn't make that call.'

'Alby thinks you might be able to figure out what's going on with the tape,' Grace said. 'He reckons you're the best.'

Byron nodded vacantly and then shook his head. 'Poor old Harry. Julie must be pretty cut up, eh?'

I looked at him. He looked back at me.

'Sorry,' he said. 'I thought you knew they were a bit of an item.'

Well, that explained all the knock-backs to my dinner offers after a hard day with my head down at the Melbourne Uni library. Harry and Julie? Who'd have thought it? Not me, that was for certain. Maybe I was slipping.

Byron plugged a cable into the back of his cassette player. He turned on a flat-screen Apple G5 and did some fiddling. After about five minutes he handed me a small microphone. 'Say exactly what's on the tape.'

This wasn't hard. The words were burned into my brain.

Byron fiddled for another couple of minutes and then two identical overlaid displays appeared on his computer screen. He studied the peaks and troughs on the graphs and did some more fiddling.

'It's your voice,' he said finally.

'But it's not.'

'Maybe you didn't make the call, but it's definitely your voice. An expert cut-and-paste job.'

I didn't say anything.

'You know that girl at the railway station with the warm and friendly voice who tells you what train is next and all the stations it's going to?' he asked.

I nodded.

'Well, she sits in a recording studio one day and reads out lots of single words and names and then they glue them all together digitally. So from one day of recording they can make her say anything and put together any kind of schedule they want, any time they need to.'

I nodded again. 'But could they have had her invite Harry out for coffee in Double Bay?' I asked.

'That's a bit trickier,' Byron said.

'But possible?'

'Oh, yeah. You can actually build up any missing words you need syllable by syllable. It was done with that bloke on the beer commercials, remember? They took thirty-year-old recordings of his voice-overs and rebuilt them. Eleven years after he died he was doing new ads for Vic Bitter.'

'And that's what happened here?' Grace asked.

'You got it. Someone got hold of some voice recordings of Alby and made up that message by isolating words and even the individual syllables. When it's all put together properly no-one can tell the difference. 'Cept a smart bugger like me, of course.' He pointed to the display on the computer screen. 'It's those little glitches on the peaks of the graphs that give it away.'

'Easy as that?' Grace asked.

'Mate,' Byron smiled, 'I almost got this really crook actress an AFI award once. By the time I finished tweaking her tapes people thought she was the next Cate Blanchett.'

'Who can do a job like that?' Grace asked.

Byron shrugged. 'Any halfway decent audio postproduction house. But to do it properly they'd need access to a fair whack of high-quality voice tapes. And this was a pretty good effort.'

'Could they do it in-house at D-E-D?' Grace asked.

Byron nodded. 'Definitely. And like I said, it's a quality job.'

I didn't like this one little bit. And Grace had asked the question I hadn't wanted to. At D-E-D we were debriefed after each mission using digital audio tapes for subsequent transcription. Back at the office they had hours and hours of my voice.

Byron popped the cassette out of the machine and handed it to me. 'So what the hell's going on?' he asked.

'You'll be the first to know when I figure it out,' I said.

Grace picked up her briefcase. 'We were never here.'

Byron nodded. He dragged the image on the computer screen to the trashcan logo and selected 'Delete'. 'I'll reformat that drive and record music over it a few times, just to make sure you're totally erased.'

I nodded. It was definitely the smart thing to do, but I really wished he could have phrased the last bit some other way.

ELEVEN

While Grace drove I checked out the contents of the envelope Armando had been keeping safe for me. Five thousand dollars in greenbacks, a New Zealand passport with my photograph and someone else's name, and a wallet with a driver's licence and enough personal detail to back up the passport. Since the Kiwis had chosen to steer an independent and humanistic path through world affairs their passports tended to be welcome most places. It was also genuine enough not to ring any bells in those countries where it would get a bit of extra scrutiny because of those same independent and humanistic policies.

They may have been 'alert but not alarmed' over at the passenger terminals but the airfreight security bods were a little more laid-back. We parked in a crowded area of the airfreight lot and sent a text message of the vehicle's location to Armando before locking the car and tucking the keys into the exhaust pipe.

Grace led the way into the office of one of the larger American airfreight companies and asked for Mr Ledbetter. A confused clerk couldn't place any Ledbetter in the company but when Grace got him to check with the duty manager things suddenly got a whole lot friendlier.

The duty manager locked his office door once we were inside. He offered us coffee but I sensed an underlying implication that we could also have his first-born child if we so wished. Grace countered the coffee suggestion with one of her own and within five minutes, dressed in grey overalls and orange safety vests, we were carrying air express priority satchels onto a tired-looking DC-10 configured for freight. This Mr Ledbetter, whoever the hell he was, certainly had some pull. The duty manager just couldn't seem to do enough for us.

The international airfreight business had grown out of the aftermath of World War II with ex-military pilots setting up small airlines using war-surplus planes. In Asia especially there was a lot of dodgy but very lucrative business to be done and these cowboy operations dovetailed nicely with the expanding postwar OSS and later CIA forays into the politics of the region. Obviously in these days of the War on Terror certain links were still being maintained.

The US-government-appointed sky marshal scheduled to fly on this leg of the freighter's travels was wary of our presence but after a brief discussion with the freight line's duty manager and the pilot and Grace's flashing of a laminated card and her Browning pistol, he packed his gear and walked off the plane. He seemed happy enough; having to overnight in Sydney on expenses is never a bad thing. Apparently my new best buddy Grace was now the acting sky marshal on this flight.

Flying shotgun must be a crappy job on freighters. With no passengers to hijack the plane you're left with watching the pilots to make sure they don't go a bit wobbly and try to prang the aircraft into some American asset somewhere. Interesting job. If the pilot looks like he means to crash the plane you have to shoot him to stop him crashing the plane. The logic was scary but what was scarier still was that there was a government somewhere run by people who actually thought it was logical.

There were half-a-dozen seats for couriers or aircrew deadheading between ports, but on this leg it was just the two of us. We strapped ourselves in and the plane was airborne just after five in the afternoon. The schedule had us on a nonstop to Singapore. While Grace was unpacking her briefcase I asked for a look at the laminated card. The high cheekbones made her photograph well. The name on the card was Mary Travers. I made a mental note to ask her later what Peter and Paul were up to these days.

The card was similar to several I'd seen in souvenir shops in Ho Chi Minh City after the war, along with corroded American dog-tags and bayonets and other battlefield detritus. Issued by the Military Assistance Command, Vietnam, or MACV, to members of something called the Studies and Operations Group, they were nicknamed 'Get Out of Jail Free' cards. The card made it very clear that the bearer was not to be detained or questioned and was authorised to wear civilian clothing, carry unusual personal weapons, and transport and possess prohibited items. They were also allowed to go anywhere, do anything and use any US government facilities, equipment and personnel they felt necessary to achieve their ends. A cheery postscript was that if the bearer was killed the card was to be left on the body. Apparently the bearer in 'Nam was usually a young, fit guy with a crew cut, wearing civvies and carrying a nifty 9mm Swedish K submachine gun. They could have really just worn T-shirts with 'Special Ops' or 'CIA' in big letters on the back.

I didn't even know I'd gone to sleep until I woke up four hours out of Sydney. I felt like death. Sleeping is no fun on a regular airline but a freighter really is something else. There was no sign of Grace so I used the opportunity to check out the Browning Hi-Power which she'd left sitting on top of her briefcase. She'd obviously been well trained since the weapon was in Condition One with the hammer cocked, safety engaged, a full magazine and a round ready in the chamber. Even up here she was prepared for trouble. The weapon was perfectly maintained and, interestingly, had no serial number or any other identifying marks. Not that the number had been filed off. Modern metallurgical techniques mean a filed-off serial number can always be recovered. This gun had never ever had a serial number so it was completely untraceable and unattributable. Must have made for an interesting late-night shift at the Browning factory. Someone would have done well out of the overtime.

Grace came back with coffee from the freighter's galley and the lunch box from Buon Ricordo. She was wearing an old US Navy pattern flying jacket, Vietnam era, about six sizes too big. Borrowed from one of the crew, I guessed.

'What's the scoop on the Bali diversion?' I asked. 'Do they reckon they can swing it without too much drama?'

It was a good year since I'd been to Bali and my body and soul could really do with a recharge. And some time to think things through without the distraction of dodging bullets.

'I had a talk to the crew,' she said with a smile. 'I'm usually fairly persuasive but I think it was Armando's zucchini frittata that clinched it.'

What a pisser. Her 'go-anywhere-do-anything-get-out-of-jail-free' card would have been enough. I was really looking forward to that frittata. Luckily there were plenty of other interesting morsels to keep me happy. Armando had outdone himself again.

But the freighter's coffee was dreadful. It always amazes me that science and engineering can produce a two-hundred-ton object capable of travelling effortlessly through the air at six hundred miles an hour with three hundred people aboard, but a decent cup of high-altitude coffee is still unattainable.

Grace just nibbled but I felt her watching me and when I looked across she smiled.

'You Aussies sure love to eat a lot,' she said.

She pronounced it 'oss-ies' like most Americans do.

'It's "OZ-ies",' I said, 'and just so you know, it's "Brizb'n" and "Melb'n". And yes, we are serious about our food. It's you Yanks who like to eat, a lot. We go for quality, not quantity.'

'Yeah, right. I tried a dim sim in Melb'n and a pie floater in Sid-Knee.' She grimaced. 'You ever tried the clam chowder or crab cakes in Baltimore? That's in Mary-Land, ya know.'

She had me there. Twice. They were both low blows. I laughed. I can be a good loser. And I'd eaten at Charlie Trotter's restaurant in Chicago. When they really want to the Yanks can actually turn on a quality feed.

'Got any kind of a handle on what might be going on yet?' she asked, munching on a stuffed mushroom.

I shook my head. With a little less pressure I might come up with something so I was looking forward to landing at Denpasar.

'They killed Harry and they tried to kill you,' she said, 'so that's the only link we have to work on. Anything else that connects you?'

'Just the Springs thing, and the fact that I helped him get his leg over on New Year's Eve.'

'A jealous husband?'

I shook my head again. 'Everyone at WORLDPIX gets a high-level vetting, same as the people at D-E-D. Harry's squeeze in Accounts would have to be Mafia-connected to justify that kind of hit and if she was she wouldn't be working for us.'

'Guess that leaves us with the Bitter Springs connection,' she said.

That was how it was starting to look to me and I'd already made up my mind to try and get a call through to Julie back in Melbourne. I had her mobile number, which would be marginally harder to tap than her home phone. Maybe I could find a more circuitous route to make contact. Then she'd be able to call me back on a secure line. Better to keep everything unofficial just for the moment until I could figure out exactly where I stood.

'I might try and grab some shut-eye,' Grace said. She handed me the pistol. 'I'm deputising you. If the pilot goes crazy you can shoot him.'

'Don't you think *I'd* have to be crazy to shoot him while he's flying the plane?' I asked.

'Good point, but since I've just deputised you you'll have to shoot yourself if you go crazy.'

I don't think she was serious but she said it with a straight face.

Grace plugged in the earpieces from her iPod and curled up, resting the briefcase on the seat next to her for safekeeping. She needn't have worried. I wasn't going to rifle through it since I'd already had a quick squiz while she was in the cockpit. Under the files on me and her there was another one.

I didn't have time to check it out but the name on the outside of the folder was enough. Even just knowing a file on me was snuggled up next to a file on Sheldon Asher really gave me the creeps.

TWELVE

The freighter pilot was a pro. He called in a disturbingly authentic-sounding mayday to Bali's Ngurah Rai airport, shut down his portside engine and two hours later we lumbered into Denpasar with the plane yawing at an alarming angle. We were back in our civvies and belted into the jump seats in the cockpit at the pilot's suggestion. It was a good suggestion. In the cockpit things were slightly less scary since we could see the pilot had total control. The plane hit the runway with a thud and slewed dramatically when the reverse thrust kicked in. We finally pulled up, tyres smoking, right at the end of the runway, where the concrete stops and the salt water takes over. Several Balinese fishermen waved happily to the crew who waved back. It doesn't hurt to be friendly when you're only twenty-five feet apart.

The pilot taxied us slowly back to the terminal, where he carefully misunderstood the instructions from the control tower and parked right next to an Air Paradise 737. Luckily for us, due to a problem with the aerobridges, the 737 was spewing its cargo of Australian holiday-makers onto the tarmac, so we mingled and made our way to Immigration. It was just on dusk and the fading light made it a little easier for us to blend in.

I scooped up some frangipani from the pathway and with those behind our ears we looked like just another couple of tourists. Those aerobridges had ruined Ngurah Rai airport for me. Disembarking at the top of the mobile stairs to a blast of humid air and the smell of jet fuel and frangipani off the tarmac is the only way to arrive in Bali. Having no luggage might have been a minor problem at customs but the copilot had handed over his personal carryall. We were unarmed again since Grace had left the Browning onboard, probably with strict instructions that the pilot should shoot himself if he felt he was beginning to behave erratically.

The arrivals hall was familiar and welcoming with its frenetic Asian bustle and noise, the wonderful mix of characters and the pervading smell of the local clove-scented Kretek cigarettes. Grace and I joined separate queues for the long, slow shuffle up to the immigration desk. I made the quick mental switch to surveillance mode and began casually but carefully clocking the waiting immigration officials and police. I was looking for any signs of increased watchfulness and perhaps a more careful than usual checking of faces against photographs in travel documents. Everything looked normal, which is exactly the feeling you should have when you're arriving 'home'.

I'd fallen in love with Bali on that first trip to Asia when I was barely nineteen. For all my bitching about Melbourne I was actually born and raised there. I'd dabbled in photography in high school and got a job in a commercial studio at the age of seventeen. Photography, I discovered, was something I had a flair for, and I was the studio's rising star until I fell madly, deeply and passionately in love with a model. When it all went sour after six months my depression cast such a pall of gloom over the studio that my boss, Case, finally decided he had to act. Case was a Dutchman who'd served as a conscript in postwar Java fighting against Sukarno's army of national liberation, and he had a bit of a soft spot for me and for the Javanese. One Monday morning he handed over a bag full of Nikons, a box of film and an airline ticket to Jakarta, with strict instructions that I wasn't to come back without a cheerier disposition and enough great pictures to fill a dozen travel brochures aimed at Indonesia's rapidly growing tourist market. It turned out to be the perfect prescription.

Bali had been the last stop on the journey but by the time I reached the magical island my introduction to Asia had blown away all the depression and the mental dullness that only a failed first love affair can produce. After a month in Java, travelling on local buses, eating at roadside food stalls and staying in small guesthouses, my high-school Indonesian had improved to the point where I could get by in almost any situation.

In Yogyakarta I linked up with a handsome young American couple I met at a bar near my hotel. Jake was wholesome, clean scrubbed and crew-cut, in permanent-press chinos and a bri-nylon short-sleeved shirt, and Linda was blonde, equally wholesome and appeared to hang on Jake's every word. They invited me to join them in their jeep on the drive to Surabaya, and along with visiting the usual monuments and ruins, we seemed to stop in on a lot of high-ranking police officers and senior-level regional government officials.

I initially thought that Jake and Linda might have been trying to recruit me into some kind of threesome – I'd seen *Jules et Jim* at the Melbourne Uni Film Society more than once. As is usually the case, the truth turned out to be even more bizarre. After a drunken night in a coastal town called Pelabuhanratu, I realised they were actually trying to recruit me as a stringer for the CIA. They worked out of the US Embassy in Jakarta and I suppose happening on a lone traveller with photographic skills and a working knowledge of Bahasa Indonesia was a lucky break for them. I was intrigued by the offer, and certainly tempted – I'd also seen *In Like Flint* a couple of times and thought I bore a more-than-passing resemblance to James Coburn, in the right light. But in the end, I guess, I really couldn't see myself in chinos and bri-nylon shirts.

Though I'd started my journey across Java in a gloomy mood, the sights, sounds, smells, tastes, music, history and culture immediately began to blast the misery and angst right out of me. Every time I hear the solid *clunk* of the shutter on an old Nikon I'm reminded of that extraordinary trip and of the lovely Javanese girl called Dinah.

Our final stop before the short flight from Surabaya to Bali was a once glamorous mountain resort from Dutch colonial days, which now had a sad air of neglect and decay about it. Saturday night found us at the hotel's 'Borobodur Nightclub' and Jake, who'd taken my rejection of a career in the spy game in good spirit, took me aside and warned me that any dalliance with the 'hostesses' had the potential to produce an extremely unwelcome medical outcome.

The nightclub took its cue from Rick's Bar in *Casablanca*, except instead of Sam at the piano there was a long-haired band from Jakarta playing AC/DC covers. They were surprisingly good on 'Highway to Hell' – especially the Angus look-alike – but the locals were hugely unimpressed and no-one danced till a cool Filipino combo struck up a little Glenn Miller, causing a stampede onto the dance floor and some very elegant two-stepping.

A curvaceous Sundanese prostitute, whom Jake nicknamed Juicy Lucy, soon had me trapped in a booth and began breathlessly offering tantalising promises of 'six to nine' or 'sex tonight'. A thick accent made it difficult to understand her but either prospect was quite terrifying.

Salvation arrived in the shape of her friend Dinah, who was short and slender and ineffably beautiful. I was smitten. To my astonishment the attraction seemed to be mutual.

Furious eye contact and profligate handholding soon led to wild kissing in the cool darkness of the booth. Dinah and I flew through the various stages of courtship in just a few hours and she promised to meet me on the terrace of my room after midnight.

Consumed by a whirlwind of emotion, I splashed on some Brut and waited in the warm, frangipani-scented night air. The only other occupants of the terrace were some geckos who stared down at me with baleful eyes as their tongues lashed out idly to collect passing insects. My aftershave dramatically increased the number of insects flying about the terrace and I hoped the geckos were grateful. Around two o'clock, worn out by the long trip and the emotions of the evening, I fell asleep on the daybed. At four I woke to a spectacular display of lightning as an electrical storm travelled along the rim of the volcano that towered above the hotel. At half-past-five the sky began to turn pink with the dawn. Dinah, of course, never came. And strangely it felt somehow right that she hadn't, and all the pain and heartache of my first lost love drifted away with the night.

It was the perfect ending to my Javanese journey and when I landed in Bali I was fresh, alert and ready to be seduced by the unique and exquisite pleasures of the island known as 'The Morning of the Earth'. If Java was eye-opening then Bali was a revelation. Mass tourism was just beginning and the handsome and sophisticated Balinese lived simply, raising large families and crops and constantly offering thanks to their Hindu gods through exquisite forms of sculpture, painting, music and dance. I was enthralled.

Six months after getting back from this trip I came across an obliquely worded advertisement for a government department seeking people with rather obscure qualifications which happened to include 'Asian language and photographic skills'. Perhaps it was the time spent with Jake and Linda that put the idea of a career in espionage in my head, but to Case's disappointment I chucked in my job at the studio, moved to Sydney, joined the Commonwealth public service and immediately began my training as a 'Field Operative'.

The thud of an immigration officer's rubber stamp on the fake Kiwi passport brought me out of my reverie. I realised I was smiling. It was always like this when I arrived in Bali.

Once past the baggage carousels I was casually waved through the customs inspection area by a bored-looking man in a brown uniform. I walked out of the terminal into the heat and the noise and the bustle of tourists, touts and taxis to where Grace was waiting by the kerb.

THIRTEEN

The cab dropped us on the main drag in Kuta, which is where all the backpackers and young tourists head on arrival. As I paid the fare I noticed Grace was scanning the traffic for any indications that we were being followed. She gave me a brief nod and I was happy to accept her assessment that the coast was clear.

The Sari Club bombing had ripped the heart out of Kuta and the rest of Bali and then SARS and the bird flu scare had taken their toll. The tourists stayed away in droves and everybody suffered. But now finally things were starting to pick up and there was some of the old energy back on the streets.

Our clothes were rumpled from the flight and wrong for the climate so we headed into Mr Shirty on Jalan Legian. Redhi, the manager – who preferred to be called Ricky Nelson – was happy to see me and soon had us both fitted out with T-shirts, a couple of loose cotton shirts and several pairs of light pants and brightly coloured shorts. Next door we bought a slinky black bathing suit for Grace, a pair of boardies for me, sandals and fake Nikes.

To complete the picture, we picked up a touristy-looking batik carryall from a roadside stall. There was some half-hearted bargaining with the vendor just for the sake of tradition but everyone involved knew I was going to pay over the odds and be happy to do it. Some of the change from my American dollars went on a couple of phone cards from a corner shop.

I chose a café and we took a table at the back. The café had three things going for it: a public phone, a clear view of the street outside and an easily accessible rear exit. The menu was the usual mixture of east and west and the food I could see on other tables looked promising. Maybe the place had four things going for it. We went for the *saté babi*, pork satay, and my mouth started watering at the thought of it.

'I'm just going to see if I can find out anything,' I said, pulling out my phone card.

Grace nodded.

I walked across to the public phone and inserted my card. The phone rang about fifteen times before I remembered what night it was and dialled another number, which was answered straight away. There was a lot of noise at the other end and I had to ask three times.

'Mrs Templeton . . . Templeton . . . grey-haired lady . . .'

That was a bit silly since they were mostly old ladies.

'With a dog . . . a really ugly dog.'

I knew a mutt with a mug like Dougal's would stand out in a crowd.

An amplified voice loudly announced, 'Duck and dive – twenty-five,' just before the phone was picked up.

'Aye, who is it?' Under the soft Scots brogue you could tell Mrs Templeton didn't like being interrupted on bingo night.

'It's me,' I said.

There was a pause.

'Are you all right, dear?' she asked. 'I saw your poor friend on the news.'

'I'm fine, Mrs T. I just need you to do me a favour.'

There was a brief pause as 'Legs, eleven' was called and I could hear the scratch of Mrs T's pencil on her bingo card.

'A girl came to your flat,' she said after the pause. 'American. Very pretty. She gave me a long story about losing an earring. Too much detail . . . made me suspicious but I let her in anyway. Was that all right?'

'It was fine, Mrs T.'

There was another pause as 'Dirty Girty' was marked off.

'If I'd said no I think she would have just broken in when I took Dougal out to do his business, so I decided to say yes so I could keep an eye on her. You have some strange friends, dear.'

Mrs T was right on the money about that one.

'Then another two men came in the afternoon,' she went on. 'They had a key and that Sassenach Dalkeith was waiting downstairs in the car.'

I wasn't sure I liked the sound of that. Gordon had only come to visit once before, some years back when I was recovering from being chucked off a moving train, and he and Mrs T hadn't exactly hit it off.

'Working-class jump-up,' she'd sniffed with true Glaswegian disdain when he'd gone. 'There's Clydeside somewhere in that boy's past, even if he does try to talk like an English toff.'

Gordon would have been appalled to hear her call him a Sassenach. Even though he tried his best to hide his class and exact geographical origins he still wanted to be known as a Scot. He liked to wear his kilt with a swagger whenever he was invited to a formal event. I always thought it was just an excuse to wear a frock.

'Do me a favour, Mrs T,' I said. 'Don't go into my place until I get back.'

'But what about your plants?'

'I can always get more plants, Mrs T. Just trust me on this one, okay?'

There was a pause while she checked off another number and then she said, 'Yes dear, if that's what you want.'

'And I need you to call someone for me, Mrs. T. Do you still have Julie's mobile number?'

'Oh, aye, now there's a lovely wee girl, Alby. Just lovely.'

Julie had dropped work stuff off to me a few times and she'd hit it off with Mrs T right away. I could see she had plans for Julie and me.

A pause as another number echoed around the hall, 'Seventy-eight, Heaven's gate', again followed by the scratching pencil.

'Call Julie and ask if it's the Lost Dogs Home,' I said, 'then just hang up when she says you must have dialled the wrong number.'

'Is it a code, dear?' she asked.

'That's right, Mrs T. Can you do it straight away?'

'Of course, dear. Just a wee minute . . . BINGO!'

My left ear was still ringing from Mrs T's winning shout when I walked back to our table.

'Anything?'

'I just put some feelers out.' I turned my mobile on and put it on the table. 'I'll give them five minutes.'

Our food arrived and the satays looked and smelled delicious – slightly charred and glistening, on a small clay grill over a bed of glowing coconut husks. A banana leaf held a moist sticky block of rice, and a generous bowl of spicy peanut sauce was ready for dipping in. Perfect!

On that first trip to Indonesia I'd become obsessed with those small pieces of marinated meat threaded on bamboo skewers and barbecued over charcoal by street vendors. When I arrived back at the studio and raved about the delights of satay, Case gave a wicked laugh and told me yet another of his little war stories from Java. Apparently, after one particularly savage firefight his unit had been collecting weapons on the battlefield and they'd come across a familiar face. The man, who operated a popular satay stall in town, right outside their barracks, was busily slicing strips of flesh from the buttocks of dead rebels. None of the Dutchmen had ever been able to face a stick of satay after that. I told Grace the tale as I savoured each mouthful of succulent pork.

I reached for the one remaining skewer which I was sure was now mine but she beat me to it. Damn.

She happily devoured the last morsels of pork. 'Sounds like the sort of story that might be apocryphal,' she said, licking her fingers clean of the peanut sauce.

'You really think so? I always kind of thought he might have been making it up.'

It wasn't a great joke but she had the good manners to laugh. That thing about the way to a man's heart being through his stomach is crap. The very best way is laughing at his jokes.

The phone flashed once. That was the agreed signal. Julie would give me ninety seconds if I needed to find somewhere private and then try again.

I excused myself and headed into the toilets. They were grim, in a third-world kind of way, but at least they were unoccupied. The mobile flashed again and I pressed 'Answer'. She'd be using the phone she kept in her sock drawer. Julie's sock drawer was incredibly well organised. The socks were arranged by colour in neat rows and the cloned mobile phone

I'd given her as a 'just in case' was tucked under the green socks. The phone should have had an untraceable signature but even so we both knew enough to keep it short.

'Thank Christ!' she said. 'Where are you? No, sorry... I don't need to know that. I wasn't sure if you were still alive.'

'I'm sorry about Harry,' I said.

There was a short pause. 'Me too,' she said, with a catch in her voice.

'What's happening?' I asked.

'Gordon's on the phone to Shit for Brains every ten seconds,' she said, 'and your name's coming up a lot.'

'And not in praise of my many virtues, I'm guessing. Who pulled me off that plane?'

'I did.'

That was a turn-up for the books. 'I didn't know you had that kind of authority.'

'Yeah, neither did I. But I figured you'd want in on the Harry thing so I made a call.'

Julie was not only smart but also very well networked.

'Can the call be traced back to you?'

'Not in a hurry,' she said.

That was good. 'Thanks, I owe you. So does everyone else on that flight.'

'Tell me about it, that was very disturbing.'

She had that right. 'Any other disturbing news I might need to know?'

'Graeme Rutherford went out at lunchtime for his usual baked bean jaffle and got hit by a cab. It didn't stop.'

That was grim. 'Fatal?' I asked.

'He's in a coma and it doesn't look good.'

'Jesus. Was it an accident?'

'They reckon the driver must have been doing about ninety. No sign of any swerving or braking so I'd guess not. Anything else I can help with?' Julie was smart enough to keep the conversation moving.

'Grace Goodluck,' I said. 'USDOJ. Name mean anything?'

'Nope, but I'll ask around. You just keep your head down for a while and I'll see what I can find out.'

'Don't take any chances.'

'You too,' she said, and hung up.

I looked at my watch. Less then forty seconds. That would make it hard for them but not impossible. Spy satellites were sucking up every phone transmission in the world and feeding them down through the dishes at Bitter Springs into computers to scan for trigger words. Would Goodluck be one?

Back at our table Grace was finishing off the rice. She looked up as I sat down. 'More trouble?'

'You heard about my cameras?'

'Exploding on the tarmac?'

'The guy who packed them was involved in a hit and run.'

'Shit. Was he a friend?'

I nodded.

'Sorry. So, what's Step Three?' she asked.

'You sure you want to hang around?'

'We're in this together now.'

'Why?'

'Look, I investigated Harry pretty thoroughly and he came up clean. I think he was a straight shooter who walked into something he didn't understand. So I figure he was on the right side and whoever wanted him dead is on the wrong side. I think the same applies to you. Am I wrong?'

'No. I just wish I could figure out what the hell's going on.'

'Your friend in the mountains . . . is it far?'

'About an hour. But I think we should lie low somewhere around here tonight and make a move in the morning.

She nodded. 'Okay by me, we're on your turf.'

'I'm not usually superstitious but the locals reckon monsters come out at night, and believe me, Balinese folklore has got some gruesome monsters.'

'I'm not sure I didn't just see one,' Grace said.

I stared at her.

'Name Buzz Geiger mean anything to you?'

I thought about Gordon's phone call. 'Why? Who is he?'

'A freelance problem-solver . . . permanent solutions are his speciality. Ex-special forces and a guy with a really bad reputation.'

'And what's the connection?'

'I saw him sitting in the café in Double Bay just before Harry got shot.'

'You were there?'

She nodded. 'After I had a look at you I flew up to Sydney for a meeting.'

I didn't much care for the 'had a look at you' comment. It made me feel like some kind of specimen. But it explained her presence on that tram. I wondered who the meeting in Sydney was with. Sheldon was based in Sydney.

'Later I planned to accidentally bump into Harry somewhere so we could sit down and have a friendly little chat.'

'A chat with Harry wouldn't have got you anywhere. He was a pro.'

'I'm a pro too,' she said. 'Plus I'm a woman.'

I have to admit she made an excellent point.

'I followed Harry to the café in Double Bay but by the time I'd parked my car it was all over. Geiger was gone and there were cops everywhere.'

'Jesus.'

'I'm pretty sure Geiger drove past here in an SUV while you were in the head.'

Fuck, this was all getting so out of hand.

FOURTEEN

We checked into a cheap losman down a couple of back alleys from Jalan Legian. The one bed in the room looked as uncomfortable as the only chair so we drew straws and we both lost.

The bathroom had a smelly squat toilet and no bath or shower. There was a *mandi* instead, the traditional Balinese tiled tub of cold water. You're supposed to soap up and then use a dipper to pour water from the tub over yourself. It's an efficient system except for those times when you really want to wallow under a continuous spray of steaming hot water. Like now.

Grace splashed about in the bathroom for a while and then came out wearing one of the white cotton shirts. Since they're intended for the tropics the cotton is very, very light and when you put one of them on over a wet body it tends to cling. And get a bit transparent. I took my turn in the bathroom and sluiced myself down. The brick and tile construction of a *mandi* keeps the water icy cold and after seeing Grace in that shirt the shock of the chilled water was exactly what I needed.

She was still wide awake when I came out of the bathroom. The shirt had dried off a little, which I was grateful for. It wasn't a great night for sleeping and even on the FAST setting our ceiling fan barely moved. The icing on the cake was a family of rats warming up for an all-night speedway race meeting round the top of the walls, under the eaves of the thatched roof.

'So tell me about Mungo?' Grace asked.

'He didn't get a whole chapter in my file?'

She shook her head. 'Just a side-note as a possible contact.'

The Honourable Munro Godfrey Rouse Vereeker Standish, or Mungo to his friends, deserved much more than a side-note but in this case I was very glad that was all he had. Mungo was a titled Pom, scion of landed gentry in Dorset, and he'd been destined from birth for a place at Eton, then the Royal Military College, Sandhurst, and a commission in the Guards. At Sandhurst there'd been a kafuffle about a liaison between young Cadet Officer Standish and a senior officer's wife and Mungo's commission and career in the Guards had gone down the gurgler. He joined the Parachute Regiment as a squaddy and a natural ability for handling himself in tight corners got him noticed by MI6.

In the sixties he'd gone into Sarawak several times, freelancing with the SAS during the 'Konfrontasi' period between Malaysia and President Sukarno's Indonesia.

On one of these patrols his team had bumped into a bunch of Indonesian RPKAD commandos, the forerunners of today's Kopassus special forces, and when the shooting was all over there were only two survivors, Mungo and an Indonesian lieutenant – both of them badly wounded. It was obvious that the jungle would finish them off so they agreed to halt the war temporarily and then dragged each other to safety. It took twelve days to reach a mission station on the river, by which time they'd become life-long buddies. Mungo went back to the SAS and was eventually pensioned off after he got himself blown up in the Falklands behind the Argentine lines attempting something nasty he was really way too old to be doing.

Retirement in Dorset on an MOD pension wasn't really Mungo's scene. The Indonesian lieutenant from the 'Konfrontasi' days was by now a major-general with many private business interests across Indonesia and a lot of pull in the military-run government. It only took one phone call from Mungo to get the ball rolling. Within a month he was limping off a Garuda jet in Denpasar with a permanent residency stamp in his passport and the deeds to a rundown restaurant and bar outside Ubud in his pocket.

The MOD pension that was laughable in Britain was quite an acceptable income by Balinese standards and Mungo took to wearing a sarong and rapidly developed the appearance of someone who'd drunk too many G and Ts and read too much Maugham. It was soon obvious that Mungo had gone totally 'troppo'. Then, to the consternation of his relatives back in Dorset, he married a beautiful young Balinese woman named Nina.

After renovating and doubling the size of the bar and restaurant, Nina methodically organised the construction of a dozen simple guest cottages with traditional *alang-alang* thatched roofs. The cottages were scattered down the hillside and near the bottom was a small spring-fed swimming pool. Mungo and Nina had two kids by this stage and another was on the way, much to Nina's delight. The Balinese love big families since the more kids you have the more certain you are of having a very large and very expensive cremation ceremony organised for you after your death. Mungo wasn't too fussed about his cremation but the hotel rooms would provide the income to feed his expanding family and the large circle of close relatives that came with his wife.

I gave Grace just enough of the story for her to know that Mungo was a safe bet for a warm welcome and an understanding ear. It was getting late by this stage and since there was just a simple latch keeping our room secure I dragged the wooden chair in front of the door and settled into it for what would be a long night. Grace took pity on me and tossed me the only pillow before she flicked off the lights.

I tried to put the pieces together but it was difficult and

I knew I didn't have all the pieces. Being in a strange country and not knowing who you can trust is part of the job. Being on your home turf and in the same situation is disconcerting. On a personal level I'd completely missed the Julie and Harry thing. That wasn't a good sign. Was I slipping? And someone wanted me out of the way so badly that they were willing to blow up a planeload of Hong Kong–bound passengers. Plus the fake message on Harry's answering machine and poor old Graeme on his near-fatal quest for that baked bean jaffle. Then there was Sheldon and Gordon's boys' club; the two of them with their heads together at every possible opportunity always made me uncomfortable. And was the Buzz that Grace recognised in Double Bay the same Buzz that had been on the phone to Gordon? And had Grace really seen him in that SUV outside the restaurant? Jesus. It was all so crazy.

I drifted off just before the ubiquitous Bali rooster started crowing and woke to find Grace already dressed and doing sit-ups. I briefly considered joining her in a show of solidarity but then she switched to push-ups and I could see I was outclassed. When she reached one hundred and started doing push-ups on her fingertips I pulled the pillow over my head.

FIFTEEN

The streets were full of bright-eyed, squeaky-clean schoolkids in neatly pressed uniforms who made me feel like a bit of a derelict, even in my new clothes. Grace had pulled off that girl trick of using a damp cloth, a comb and the flat of her hand to make herself look like a million bucks. We accepted the first shouted query of 'Transport? Transport?' from a man in a Suzuki minivan and asked to be driven across the island to the beachfront hotel strip in Sanur.

Even though it was still early the roads were crammed with trucks and vans and bemos and any empty space between these vehicles was filled up with motor scooters. Some of the scooter drivers looked to be about twelve and every so often we passed a family of five or six all neatly balanced on a straining 100cc motor bike. Teenage schoolgirls in light blouses and dark skirts, their arms filled with textbooks, casually rode side-saddle as their friends nimbly cut in and out of the steadily flowing traffic and Bali went about its morning business, ignored by the local police.

In Sanur I had the driver turn into the entrance of the Tanjung Sari Hotel and drop us halfway down the drive.

We checked in and I booked the Honeymoon Suite with Grace hanging off my hip like a besotted sixteen-year-old. Inside the room we closed all the shutters and dummied up a couple of figures under a sheet on the king-sized bed, using spare pillows and rolled-up towels from the bathroom. When the coast was clear I put a *Do Not Disturb* sign on the door and we ambled down to the beach and headed south for some breakfast.

Even if Grace had been mistaken about seeing Buzz Geiger in the SUV the previous night, Julie's account of the goings-on back at D-E-D still had me rattled. Whoever wanted me dead wasn't going to be far behind and there was no point in making it easy for them.

The Bali Hyatt stretches lazily along the beach, set discreetly back amongst palm trees and acres of lush tropical gardens. Built thirty years ago, the joint is on the verge of turning into a classic, like Raffles in Singapore or the Royal Hawaiian on Waikiki. I keep waiting for them to renovate it into blandness but so far they seem to have resisted the temptation.

At the beachside pool an advance guard of German tourists was methodically annexing the best of the sun lounges with beach towels. Grace hung back and started up a conversation with one of them so she could watch my back as

I checked out the restaurant. Once I was seated and she was sure the coast was clear she joined me at a table on the terrace. We had a lovely view over the lotus pond, but more importantly a clear line of sight to the hotel lobby and the path from the beach.

Grace had muesli with fruit and yoghurt. I resisted the temptations of the eggs cooked to order and the sausages and the bacon and the pancakes and the sautéed potatoes and the pastries and got myself a fruit plate and a bowl of Nutri-Grain. Those fingertip push-ups of Grace's had shaken me rigid.

I was fascinated by two slender, gorgeous-looking eastern European teenage girls at the next table as they petulantly ignored their muscle-bound boyfriends and hoovered their way steadily across the entire breakfast buffet. Maybe pouting keeps you thin.

Grace was transfixed by a graceful young Balinese girl in an elegant sarong and kebaya carrying a tray of offerings on her head. The girl knelt every so often to gently place small woven baskets on the pathways. Her movements were delicate and mesmerising.

'That's beautiful. What's she doing?'

'They're offerings,' I explained. 'Part of everyday life for the Balinese. Usually the baskets contain flowers, incense and a little bit of food, like rice or biscuits. They're to give pleasure to the gods and to persuade the demons to leave you alone. They also provide good karma to the people involved in their preparation.'

'I thought Indonesians were Muslims,' Grace said.

'Most of them are but the Balinese aren't. They have their own brand of Hinduism with a touch of animism.'

This triggered a lot of questions from Grace about the Balinese and their rituals and beliefs which I answered as best I could. I'm no expert and it's an endlessly complex subject but I was happy to share what I knew about these amazing people. I was surprised that a US Army captain was listening with rapt attention as I spoke of black and white magic and the Balinese belief of contacting the other world through transmediums. But she was. Grace was shaping up to be an interesting package.

After a pot of *kopi bali* we paid the bill and walked through the lobby with its soaring thatched roof and down the long drive to the main drag, Jalan Tamblingan.

We hired a car and driver from outside the Hyatt and headed out to the village of Mas, where Bali starts to climb up towards the mountains. We paid off the driver near a road junction and killed twenty minutes at a wood carver's like the regular tourists, then flagged down a local bus for the ride to the mountain village of Ubud and Mungo's Bar.

We went the back way, up through Sayan, and Grace was entranced by the scenery. It was market day so we shared the bus with housewives loaded down with baskets of vegetables and trussed chickens, and a slender Javanese with pockmarked skin who was thinking of picking my pocket until he looked in my eyes and saw I was thinking of breaking his fingers. We drove through tiny villages with their main-road souvenir shops and high-walled family compounds, and past numerous abandoned-looking temples.

I explained to Grace that the temples would spring back into vibrant, noisy and colourful life as soon as the next religious festival came up on the complex Balinese ritual calendar. The buildings would be restored and cleaned, purified by the priests and decorated with flags and banners and colourful umbrellas shading the stone carvings of various gods. These gods, wrapped in the black-and-white chequered cloths that symbolise the constant struggle between good and evil, would have offerings of flowers and rice and incense heaped before them.

It would be great if the struggle between good and evil were as clearcut as those black-and-white sarongs. In my world there were only shades of grey, and right now everything was tending towards charcoal, like the storm clouds I could see gathering in the distance over Agung, the sacred mountain.

Out along the narrow, palm-fringed roadway we passed terraced mountainside fields ripe with the rich green shoots of a new rice crop and children chattering and splashing in ponds and roadside canals. Occasional flocks of squawking ducks waddled along the roadway, each group marshalled by a farmer using a feather on the end of a long bamboo pole to guide them. They were headed out for a day of foraging in the wet rice fields for slugs and beetles, and in the wonderful balance of nature that is so Balinese the ducks would be fertilising the fields while acting as a natural pesticide.

We passed small groups of elegant and beautifully dressed women walking to local temples with tall and colourful offerings of fruit, cakes and flowers balanced gracefully on their heads. If you have to hide out some place, Bali has a lot going for it.

Mungo's Hotel & Restaurant was a simple bamboo and clay-brick affair just outside Ubud with a terrace restaurant overlooking a hundred-foot drop into the Tjampuhan River valley. To the right you could sometimes just make out the ocean miles away, and to the left, through the clouds, a line of volcanoes ran off into the distance. The valley itself was the average Bali view of spectacular emerald-green rice terraces spilling down the steep hillsides, coconut palms and lush jungle, with the occasional family compound or shrine. In the late afternoons the river teemed with families washing their clothes, their kids, their water buffaloes and themselves. At night through the blackness you'd see the light of fires from the surrounding villages and sometimes hear the sound of gamelans playing. This was Mungo's view every day of the year, poor bugger.

The hand-lettered sign by the entrance to the hotel read CLOSED FOR RENOVATIONS. That usually meant Nina and the kids had gone back to her home village for a temple festival and Mungo didn't want to be pestered by drop-ins looking for a room. He was hard at work relaxing in a hammock slung between two palm trees near the pool and glanced up from his book when we crunched down the long gravel driveway from the road.

'Alby, dear boy,' he drawled, 'what a treat. Give Wayan a shout, would you? Tell him to get the cookboy to sling some Bintang on ice and slaughter the fatted calf. I'd get up and greet you properly, and the young lady, but all this page turning has fair worn me out.'

He did get up out of the hammock though, rather awkwardly given his bum leg, and gave me a hug and then gave Grace a bigger one. If I'd been all by myself I doubt if he'd have made the effort.

Wayan was the hotel's manager but he was also a talented wood carver and had a small shop next to the reception area. He came from a large family of painters and wood carvers and the shop was full of examples of their work.

Wayan came out of the small office when he heard our voices and beamed at me. We shook hands and I introduced Grace. He beamed at her too, and I noticed he spent a long time studying her face.

Madé, the 'cookboy' in Mungo's politically incorrect and imperialist parlance, also joined us and embraced me like a long-lost brother. He was about fifty and had trained as a chef in the kitchens of one of the international hotel chains before getting a stint in their five-star flagship operation in Paris. The cold and homesickness brought him back to Bali after only six months and Nina used a family connection to lure him to Mungo's kitchen. He served us cold drinks on the terrace and announced he would prepare a special lunch. I suggested something light, which seemed to disappoint him, but he brightened up when I pointed out we would be in for dinner.

Wayan was hovering about and I saw him staring at Grace when he thought no-one was watching. But then again she was worth staring at.

Madé's lunch, a steaming hot chicken and noodle soup called *soto ayam*, was delicious and 'just in case' Madé had put out prawn satay and some *tum bebek*, small steamed parcels of spiced minced duck wrapped in banana leaf. Grace nursed one of the local Bintang beers, switching to lime squash when she finished it, which was a good sign. Keeping your wits about you was a virtue I admired. Of course, letting your hair down when it was appropriate was something I could also appreciate in a woman.

As we ate I gave Mungo a quick run-down on what had brought us to his door. The limp might have slowed him down a bit but his brain was as fast as ever. He immediately said he would have Nina extend her stay at the family compound and then he'd keep the hotel closed for as long as we needed a place to hide out. I offered him some cash to cover the loss of income but he refused, just as I knew he would. I decided to leave the cash under the office door when we left, just as he knew I would.

'I'll call Nina now,' Mungo said, getting up from the table.

'You know, I might even take this opportunity to actually do some of those renovations.'

I for one wouldn't be holding my breath.

'So tell me,' I said, finishing the last of the satays, 'exactly when did Harry's name pop up in your missing aeroplane investigation?'

'Aeroplane?' Grace said.

'Sorry, "airplane" in your language. And they used to land at aerodromes before we caved in and started calling them airports.'

'Aerodromes I like,' she said, unwrapping one of the banana-leaf parcels. 'You guys shouldn't cave in so easy. Anyway, I was looking for missing Globemasters and Harry was looking at a place where Globemasters were landing on a regular basis. He made a back channels inquiry about the base at Bitter Springs. It's theoretically resupplied by a regular AMC Globemaster run out of Guam and any Globemaster queries were red-flagged back to me.'

'Theoretically?'

'The supply flights were evidently contracted out some time back to a private company, but everything I did to try and track down the private contactors hit a brick wall. So when Harry's red-flagged query popped up I decided to attack it from that angle.'

'But the Springs personnel vetting he was working on is just a biannual exercise in rubber-stamping,' I said.

She shrugged. 'Well, something got him killed.'

I thought about it for a while. 'Harry was a bit of a party animal and a joker,' I said, 'but he was a terrier for detail. If something fishy had come up in the vetting he'd have gone after it.'

She nodded. 'And if he was sticking his nose in where it wasn't wanted... and you were supposed to be working on the assignment with him, then you'd be a liability as well.'

I really didn't like this. Not too many people knew I was supposed to be working with Harry on the vetting. And the people who did know should have been on my side.

'What about you?' I asked.

'What *about* me?'

'Haven't you been sticking your nose in the same places as Harry?'

She smiled. 'That's why I wanted to get out of town for a bit.'

'You took that tape from Harry's answering machine, right?' I asked.

'When I realised Harry was down I hightailed it over to his place to give it a quick toss before anyone else could. I grabbed the tape and then headed to your place to give it the once-over.'

'Since I was on a plane to Hong Kong.'

She nodded, then stopped, shook her head and smiled ruefully. Not a whole lot of people outside the D-E-D office would have known about my travel plans.

'You got me there,' she said. 'Nicely done.'

'I'm a pro too,' I said. 'Plus I'm a man.'

She laughed. 'So anyway, your very friendly neighbour, Mrs Templeton, let me in.' She smiled. 'I said I'd lost an earring but I don't think she bought it.'

'She didn't. Too much detail gave you away.'

'Damn!'

'Discover anything interesting?' I asked.

She shook her head. 'Just that you need to change the dustbag in your vacuum cleaner. Then I looked out the window and saw you get out of a cab.'

So that face at the window hadn't been Mrs T's.

'A minute later two heavies on a Yamaha pulled up and went after you.'

'And you followed?'

'It looked like it might get interesting.'

'And you sent me the tape?'

Grace nodded. 'I gave a surfie kid five bucks to drop it off. I just wanted to see your reaction but then things started getting out of hand.'

'Nice of you to intervene.'

'When you're in the middle of a routine investigation and your persons of interest start getting whacked it's time to get pro-active. I winged the shooter on the street and tried to head off the other one waiting up the hill.'

That explained the squeal of tyres I'd heard as I headed out the back door of the café.

'So we agree the common link in all this is the Springs?' I asked.

'Looks like it.'

'I just can't see what the connection is,' I said.

'Me neither, yet.'

There was a pot of coffee over a warmer and I poured a cup and offered her some.

'No thanks, I need to clear my head. I'm going to do some laps in that lovely-looking pool and then take a nap.'

Grace took a lot of naps. Harry used to have a cat named Tiger who took a lot of naps. That was all Tiger seemed to do, eat and sleep. Then one day I saw him spring a good two metres into the air from a sitting position and pull down an unsuspecting pigeon as it flew past. When it was all over, there were feathers from elbow to breakfast in Harry's garden and Tiger was back snoozing contentedly under a lillipilli. Maybe there was something in this napping business.

SIXTEEN

Around 5 p.m. I knocked on Grace's door. With the hotel at zero per cent occupancy we had a wide choice of rooms and she'd taken one near the pool. She was dressed in a batik sarong and was towelling her hair dry when she came to the door. The swim and the nap had worked their magic and she was glowing. I hated being the bearer of bad news.

'You were right about seeing Geiger.'

'Shit. I'd rather have been wrong. Are you sure?'

'Yep. Mungo knows him. And he agrees with your personality assessment.'

'How the hell did he get onto us so quickly?'

'He didn't. He's got a house down in Seminyak. This is where he drops out between contracts. He arrived in Bali before we did so he's not following us.'

'I wouldn't count on that for too long,' Grace said.

'Agreed. It's too close for comfort.'

'So what are our exit options?'

'Well,' I said, 'our friendly cargo freighter is long gone and I've got a funny feeling that the airports might be under tighter surveillance than when we arrived.'

'How about by sea?'

'Ferries to the other islands leave from Benoa, Padang Bai and Celuk Bawang. Or you can cross to Java by ferry from Gilimanuk. But they're all busy ports and all easily watched.'

'Fishing boat?'

'A bit risky for a long trip in open water.'

'What about a charter? I've got my skipper's ticket.'

Of course she did. 'Too much paperwork. But you're on the right track. There's always a lot of yachties cruising these islands. Grace Goodluck, we're going to a dance.'

I was wearing long red shorts, walking boots I'd borrowed from Mungo, an outrageously patterned shirt, wrap-around sunglasses and an orange terry-towelling hat, so in Bali tourist terms I was almost invisible. Grace dulled herself down a bit in jeans and a plain shirt but when you're that good-looking it's tough to hide it.

As we left the hotel Wayan was coming down the driveway carrying a tray of offerings. He put the tray down before plucking a frangipani blossom from a tree and handing it to Grace. She thanked him and tucked the flower behind her ear.

'*Salamat jalan,*' he said, 'travel safely.' Then he added, 'Be careful.'

I noticed Grace looking into his eyes and nodding gently and smiling. Something was going on here and whatever it was I wasn't quite getting it.

It was a long walk down the hill and I was starting to feel the heat a little by the time we reached the Tjampuhan Hotel. Grace wasn't even breathing hard. She *had* had a nap, of course, but I'd watched her put in a hundred laps of the pool before she hit the sack. It wasn't a very big pool but she'd swum it like she was trying to qualify for the Olympics. I didn't have a stopwatch but I reckon she might have been in with a chance.

At the bottom of the hill we crossed the road and passed a small group of bemo drivers gathered round a young boy grilling satays over a portable barbecue. He fanned his charcoal fire vigorously with a square of banana leaf and smoke and the aroma of char-grilling chicken filled the air. I was tempted to join the line of drivers but Murni's was just a short walk away over the rickety weathered planks of the old suspension bridge.

Murni's had started as a simple roadside *warung* in the early seventies, back when the old bridge was the only way to cross the deep ravine where the Oos and Tjampuhan rivers meet. It was still in the same location but now it was a multi-level restaurant complex spilling down a hillside.

Grace had worked up an appetite so I introduced her to

the delights of the local deep-fried spring rolls called *lumpia goreng* and *gado gado,* a crispy salad of blanched vegetables served with prawn crackers and the ubiquitous spicy peanut dressing.

After our snack we wandered up the road and joined a group of tourists waiting outside a hotel for transportation to the dance. Arriving at the temple in a full minibus would allow us to blend in with the rest of the audience and would also give me a chance for a bit of eavesdropping. I was targeting people with weathered faces and deck shoes.

The sun sets quickly in the tropics and the light over the temple gateway changed rapidly from a warm, sunset yellow to a deep purple. Then suddenly it was dark and the waxing moon gently lit the stone carvings of gods and idols on the gateway, assisted by light flickering from a dozen blackened lamps burning palm-oil. Bats began swooping through the warm, flower-scented night air as the tourists wandered into the temple's courtyard for the evening dance performance.

According to the roneoed sheet we'd been given with our tickets, tonight's performance was the *Barong-Ket*, featuring a good-natured monster in its age-old battle with the forces of evil personified in the witch Rangda. Right now I could really identify with Mr Barong.

There were a variety of Barong dances and the *Barong-Ket*, while still sacred, is performed primarily for tourists. It was close to twenty-five years since I'd first witnessed a performance of the Barong dance in these mountains and I knew the first crashing notes of the gamelan orchestra would still make the hairs on the back of my neck stand on end as they had done then.

The audience was a mix of Americans, Europeans and Australians with one or two Japanese. They shuffled down the rows of bamboo seating as young girls from the village offered them cold soft drinks and packets of the pungent Krupuk prawn crackers. The brass keys and red and gold painted stands of the gamelan's instruments glinted in the lamplight as a white-clad temple priest, who would make the necessary offerings before the performance, chatted casually with members of the orchestra. Clove-scented cigarette smoke wafted through the air, mixing with the aroma of incense and frangipani. It was just another night in paradise but, sadly, our task was to find a way to get the hell out of there.

Grace wandered off to check out the temple architecture but I watched her and noted the professional manner in which she found all the danger points and dead ends just in case we had to make a quick exit. While scanning the crowd for anyone else scanning the crowd and any sign of danger, I noticed a good-looking middle-aged couple. They weren't too weatherbeaten but she was wearing deck shoes and he had on a spray jacket with a Royal Hong Kong Yacht Club insignia. Promising signs.

I took a seat behind them. They were explaining to a young Swedish backpacker how they'd sailed their yacht from Macau and were cruising down through the Indonesian archipelago with no fixed itinerary, just heading in a general southerly direction. Bingo! Their accents said they were Australian and they were both tanned, lean and very fit-looking. A couple of Aussies heading south in a yacht could fit in with our travel plans very nicely. Grace slipped into the seat next to me and I indicated the Australian couple. She checked them out, then nodded.

The gamelan struck up and the long-awaited Barong began its entrance through the temple gate. The hairs on the back of my neck did stand up as the first strident notes filled the air. The Barong is a hairy version of the dancing lions that stalk the streets of the world's Chinatowns during lunar New Year festivities. The creature has a long, erect tail and a large head, animated by a fantastic silver and gold painted wooden mask with bulging eyes, flaring nostrils and wildly flapping ears. A cavernous mouth is filled with sharp clacking teeth, and gorgeously painted and mirror-bedecked fabrics hang from its broad shoulders.

Our Barong tentatively peered one way and the other from the top of the temple steps, posturing with lifted bare feet and darting its head from side to side.

I glanced at Grace, who was mesmerised by the spectacle. The woman from the yacht was watching with a smile on her face, occasionally lifting a camera to her eye to quickly compose and shoot. She held her camera like someone who knew what she was doing. As my eyes flicked back and forward from her to the Barong I noticed she was gently pressing the shutter at exactly the right second to perfectly capture an expressive gesture or a dramatic pose. If she could sail as well as she could shoot pictures I'd have no problem in taking a long ocean voyage with her.

After the dance we shuffled out with the crowd, keeping an eye on the Australian couple. They were getting into a Suzuki jeep when I approached them.

'Any chance of a lift?' I asked.

The woman smiled. 'We're heading for the Tjampuhan. That any help?'

I nodded. 'We're just a bit further up the hill so the Tjampuhan would be great.'

'I'm Martin,' the man said, offering his hand, 'and this is Faith.'

Grace introduced herself as Mary Travers. She called me Mike. We shook hands all round and then Grace and I climbed into the back seat of the Suzuki.

There was the usual post-dance traffic jam so we weren't going anywhere in a hurry. Motorbikes, jeeps and bemos battled for space as a policeman with an illuminated baton tried to make order out of the chaos.

'Nice jacket, Martin,' Grace said. 'You a sailor?'

'Learning to be. We're pretty new to it but we're getting better as we go.'

'Coastal cruising or blue water?' Grace said.

'We've done a bit of blue water lately. Just got in from Macau a few days ago.'

'Wow! That's a hell of a trip. Just the two of you?'

'Yep,' Faith said. 'We've got a forty-two-footer.'

Good work, Grace. With three innocent questions she had found out almost everything we needed to know for the moment.

'Staying in Ubud for a while?' I asked.

'Probably another day or so, then we're heading back to the boat.'

Okay, we had time to work out our next move. 'Might bump into you again, then,' I said.

'Maybe,' Faith said. 'Ubud's a small place.'

Ubud *is* a small place so once we cleared the traffic jam it was a quick trip. When we got to the Tjampuhan driveway we jumped out, thanked them and headed up the hill to Mungo's. Grace set a cracking pace.

'Exactly how big is a forty-two-foot boat?' I said.

'You mean apart from being forty-two feet long?'

'Yes!'

'Big enough to take four in comfort and get you anywhere you want to go.'

'Perfect. I definitely think we're going to bump into Martin and Faith again tomorrow.'

SEVENTEEN

The walk up the hill from the Tjampuhan nearly bloody killed me but the thought of dinner kept me going. Mungo's driveway was lit with dozens of tiny flickering terracotta oil lamps and Wayan appeared to have been very busy with his offerings, which were everywhere. This latest batch were made of different coloured rice – yellow, red, white and black.

Madé had gone all out during the afternoon and now the restaurant's impressive and intricately carved sideboard held a variety of inviting dishes. He proudly guided us along the buffet: next to a conical mound of the festive yellow rice called *nasi kunning* sat a large bowl of green papaya soup and platters of minced seafood satay grilled on stalks of lemon grass, ox tongue in sweet nutmeg sauce, duck roasted in banana leaves and a whole grilled snapper. There was a bowl of fern tips with garlic and chilli for those who fancied some greens, and a variety of scorching chilli sambals along with the cooling, sweet pickled vegetables called *acar*. We were honoured by such an elaborate feast but there was so much food I had to check with Mungo to see if they were expecting a bus tour.

Madé put an insulated cooler full of Bintang, water and soft drinks by the table and Wayan positioned a fruit platter for dessert on the buffet. He took a long time to get the platter in exactly the right place and I noticed there were several offering baskets on the sideboard along with burning incense. Many more than usual.

The phone in the hotel's office rang and Mungo limped away to answer it. After making sure we had enough food to keep us going and putting a pot of coffee on a warmer, Madé wished us goodnight and left for his village.

Wayan came over to our table as soon as Madé was gone. He pulled a small leather pouch from his pocket and took out two silver rings mounted with moonstones. He solemnly placed one in front of each of us.

'I have been to see my grandfather and he says you must wear these.'

Wayan's grandfather was a renowned Balian or shaman. Balians have a range of specialities and are consulted by the Balinese on a variety of matters from health to good fortune to romance. Some operate in the hidden but very real world of Balinese magic, including black magic, and for Wayan to openly acknowledge the existence of this world to a non-Balinese meant he felt that something was seriously wrong. The rings, if they came from a Balian, were to protect us from evil influences.

Grace picked up her ring and studied it. She looked up at Wayan.

'Under the stone there is a piece of Gaharu wood from East Java. For protection.'

Grace nodded and put the ring on her middle finger. She looked down at it, rubbed the stone gently and looked back at Wayan. '*Terima kasih,* Wayan,' she said softly. Thank you.

I had a healthy respect for the powers of Balinese magic and I knew that Wayan's grandfather was a Balian Taksu, a medium who contacts the spirit world through trance. Trance is a very important part of life in Bali. It is a part of their religious ceremonies and I had seen its power. I was once urgently signalled to kneel down by the wheel of my jeep in the driveway of one of Bali's most exclusive hotels while a local youth, deeply in trance, wandered the open-air lobby conversing in tongues with the carved stone figures that dotted the forecourt, while being protected and gently shepherded by men from his village. The hotel's reception staff were also kneeling below the youth's eye level in an interesting demonstration of five hundred years of eastern mysticism colliding with a place where the rooms went for a very western five hundred bucks a night.

I put my ring on and nodded a thank you to Wayan.

'I will spend tonight meditating at the *pura dalem*,' Wayan said.

The *pura dalem* was the village death temple located near the cemetery. The Balinese believed that a night spent meditating there could either give you power over evil or wind up turning you into evil itself, perhaps in the form of a *leyak* or witch. It wasn't something a Balinese would choose to do lightly so Wayan must have been really worried about us.

He smiled and wished us a good night and not long afterwards we heard his little two-stroke scooter putt-putting up the long driveway to the road. I didn't envy him the next few hours. I figured a night in a two-star hotel was always going to be better than sitting meditating in the moonlight in the courtyard of a death temple.

After we'd made a substantial dent in the food, Mungo came back from the office. Several discreet phone calls to his contacts in Jakarta had turned up information which I was less than pleased to hear. As he talked I found myself twisting the silver ring on my finger. The moonstone felt warm.

'Word is out that you had Harry popped,' Mungo said, 'so they had a committee meeting on the thirteenth floor and put your name on a red folder.'

'Jesus!'

Mungo nodded. 'Quite so, old chap. And it gets worse, I'm afraid.'

The 'red folder' business meant anybody delivering my person or some halfway decent proof of my demise to the D-E-D office was going to score mucho brownie points. I didn't know how it could get worse than that.

'Seems like the underworld have also taken an interest in

you. There's a quarter of a million dollar price on your head. US dollars at that. At the current rate of exchange that makes you a very tempting target.'

I was reeling at this news and got up and poured myself a cup of coffee.

Grace was staring at me. 'Maybe I should cash you in and retire,' she said.

'Hold on there, Grace,' Mungo said. 'I saw him first.'

The prospect of a large amount of reward money certainly lets you know who your friends are.

'There's definitely nothing you're not telling me?' Grace asked. 'That's a hell of a lot of money in anyone's language.'

She was right about that. I couldn't figure out what was going on but I decided that if I was worth a quarter mil plus dead then I should definitely think about putting up my freelance photography rates.

Grace excused herself and headed in the direction of the Ladies'. Mungo watched her with interest. 'The CIA apparently have a bit of their own panic on,' he said. 'Sydney office has a major alert out. They're looking for a woman. No name or description, just a codename – *Mankiller*.'

'Red folder too?'

Mungo shook his head. 'Just an AOS/DNA. But it's got a priority tag.'

'Advise on sighting, do not approach' meant someone wanted to find out exactly where someone else was and the priority tag meant *Right Now*.

I looked down at the ring again. Wayan's grandfather was right on the money.

Mungo took a beer from the cooler and pulled off the cap with an opener. 'Wayan thinks she's a witch, you know.'

'A witch?'

Mungo shrugged. 'Or a spirit, or goddess or reincarnation of Sita or some such mumbo jumbo.' He took a swig of his beer. 'Haven't you noticed she looks a bit like half the wood carvings on the walls?'

I glanced around and he was right. The high foreheads and cheekbones, almond eyes and straight noses on a lot of the carvings did remind me of Grace.

'Bugger spent all afternoon making offerings and lining them up along the bloody driveway,' Mungo continued.

I felt a shiver through my bones, even though it was a balmy 25 degrees Centigrade and the chillies in the sambals had raised a sweat. I remembered that those multi-coloured rice offerings were called *Segehan* and they were placed on the ground at night in the hope of keeping demons at bay until dawn.

I was pouring a second cup of coffee when Grace came back to the table and sat down. When we finally managed to convince Mungo we'd had more than enough to eat he disappeared in the direction of his private bungalow. He came back after several minutes and put a couple of fresh sarongs and two ziplock plastic bags on the table. The larger bag held a pistol and the smaller a spare clip. The gun was a very old Russian military issue Makarov PM, with faded blueing and some signs of corrosion, but its steel clip was fully loaded with eight shiny new cartridges. The spare clip was also full. I checked the action. The Makarov might have been old but it was clean and properly lubricated. While I was grateful to Wayan for the protective rings and the offerings in the driveway I had to admit I was happier to have the gun. Although not extremely accurate or lethal at ranges beyond 15–20 metres, the old Makarov is a formidable and reliable weapon.

Grace stood up and began to help Mungo clear the table. I offered to lend a hand but she suggested I get us a key to one of the bungalows.

'Just one?' I asked.

'Let's not get overexcited,' she said. 'Given what Mungo just told us we should be more cautious. "Never split your forces in an unknown situation." Isn't that the rule? The British found that out the hard way at Isandhlwana.'

'You're worried about Zulus?' I asked. I knew all about Zulus and the British military disaster at Isandhlwana in Natal in 1873. Harry's cure for a dose of the blues was to hunker down on his couch with a bottle of Johnnie Walker and a DVD of *Zulu*, so I'd seen it more than a couple of times over the years. Plus I've always had a soft spot for Michael Caine.

She smiled. 'I'm worried about everything. Nothing makes sense,' she said, and started towards the kitchen with a pile of plates.

I wandered over to the office and got the key to the Mahwah Suite. *Mahwah* means Rose and I'd stayed in that bungalow before. It was towards the bottom of the hill, away from the noise of the road, with a spectacular view across the valley. It had two mosquito-netting-shrouded beds, plus a very comfortable day bed out on the balcony. But more importantly, there was a convenient exit path to the river in case of trouble.

I hunted out a box under the counter marked 'Lost Property', rummaged through it and found an old cassette tape Walkman. The batteries still seemed okay.

Mungo and Grace were back at the table. She handed me the gun but I decided I'd rather have her protecting my back. I'd seen how she could shoot. 'You hang onto it. Just in case all those chillies inflame my blood during the night,' I said.

Mungo looked at Grace and then at me and shook his head. 'In your dreams, matey,' he said before ambling back to his bungalow. I think he might have been laughing.

Grace picked up the sarongs and we walked to our room down a frangipani-lined path lit by more of the tiny terracotta oil lamps and a further scattering of offerings.

At any other time it would have been incredibly romantic. But a lot of people I knew were turning up dead or damaged, I was wanted by my own organisation, there was a price on my head for any crim who felt like having a crack at it, and Buzz Geiger had a bolthole 20ks away in Seminyak. Plus

I was about to spend the night with a stranger with a gun who I knew for a fact was a very good shot, and the CIA were missing a woman codenamed Mankiller. Tonight might have been a lot of things but it certainly wasn't romantic.

EIGHTEEN

As we walked towards our bungalow I watched Grace studying the layout of the hotel, checking escape routes and marking points of possible attack. I'd done this on my earlier visits out of habit, but it was reassuring to see her doing the same thing. I knew a few bods from the US Department of Justice and I wouldn't have felt comfortable with any of them watching my back. Grace was a different matter altogether.

I unlocked the padlock that secured the beautifully carved double wooden doors to our suite. These long-shanked padlocks were a Balinese hotel tradition. The key was usually attached by wire to a piece of carved and painted wood about the size of a railway sleeper. I guess this was intended to stop you taking the key with you when leaving the hotel, and it worked.

Inside the room Grace did a quick walk around and came to the obvious conclusion that the door was the major weak point. Apart, of course, from the thatched roof and the flyscreen-fitted windows. We manoeuvred a heavy carved wooden sideboard into place across the doorway. It wasn't discussed, we just did it.

'Want me to take the first watch?' she asked.

I shook my head. 'After that last cup of coffee I doubt that I'll be dozing off any time soon, so you might as well hit the sack.'

'Okay.' She looked at the beds. 'You have a preference?'

'Girls,' I said.

'Big surprise,' she said, with a smile.

After looking at the sarongs she chose one and tossed it and the pistol onto the double bed. The other sarong landed on the single bed under the window. So that was that. She gave the room a final, careful once-over, picked up her sarong, took a towel from the stack on the end of one of the beds and walked across to the bathroom.

There were three steps down from our main room into the bathroom. It was a small, stone-walled courtyard open to the sky, with a toilet in a separate alcove, a hand basin mounted on one wall and a large sunken tub with a shower head above it. And there were lots and lots of plants. If you used just a little imagination it was like showering under a waterfall out in the jungle. The room was gently illuminated by moonlight and the same tiny flickering oil lamps that lined the hotel's walkways. I assumed Wayan must have lit the lamps for us, and then with another shiver I had to ask myself how he could have known which one of all the empty rooms we would choose.

Balinese craftsmen spend a lot more time on the carving of their doors than they do working on the hinges or the locks. Just as the water started running in the shower the bathroom door creaked softly and swung slowly open. From where I was sitting I could look straight in. So I did. Naked, Grace was spectacular – lean and muscular and very, very toned. Her wet black hair and golden skin glistened in the lamplight. The plastic surgery was very good. Not her breasts, they were God-given, and obviously on a day when He was feeling particularly generous. The surgery was on the bullet wounds, two of them, on her waist, close to the left hip. Entrance wounds, by the size of the scars. She turned and began rinsing her hair. The exit wounds were bigger and even the best plastic surgery couldn't completely repair that sort of damage. She had a very beautiful arse too, I noticed, and then I figured I'd seen more than I was entitled to so I walked across the room and quietly closed the door.

When she came out of the bathroom she was wearing a light cotton shirt and her sarong, and had her hair wrapped in a towel. The sarong was tied the way the Balinese do it.

'Fantastic bathroom,' she said.

I had to agree. 'Nice job with the sarong.'

'Thanks. Wayan showed me how to do it properly.'

'I notice you decided against totally following local tradition, though.'

She nodded. 'I'm sure I'd be a lot cooler without the shirt but you need to keep your mind on the job, I'm afraid.'

Bali had been known for centuries for the beauty of its bare-breasted women and had been a magnet for seamen, travellers and adventurers because of it. The custom had almost died out now but it was a perfectly logical practice, a sensible way of dealing with life in a tropical climate. For social and religious gatherings the women wore modest but exquisitely beautiful garments but in the fields, at the markets and at home they simply went about their business bare-breasted. When the Dutch annexed the northern part of the island in the early nineteen-hundreds the new governor ordered the women to cover up to protect the morals of his soldiers. As Dutch influence spread south successive administrations tried to stamp out the custom and in the nineteen-sixties even the government of a now independent Indonesia felt bare-breasted women were not the image a sophisticated nation should be presenting to the outside world. C'est la vie.

Grace began combing her hair and it was obvious she wasn't wearing anything under the shirt. It was a sight I could live with but I decided to have a shower anyway. If she'd used up all the hot water that was going to be just fine by me.

When I came out of the bathroom the lights were out except for one small oil lamp. I was wearing my sarong.

'That was a wonderful dinner,' she said from underneath her mosquito net. 'You keep yourself trim for someone who spends so much time in pursuit of good food.'

'Eating well is the best revenge,' I said, stretching out on the bed under the window.

'For what?'

'My mum's meat and three veg when I was growing up.'

'Not a gourmet cook?'

I shook my head. 'God no. Steak or lamb chops cooked way past well done and vegetables boiled into a pulpy mass.'

'I thought *living* well was the best revenge?'

'Eating well *is* living well.'

'And you eat well?'

'Whenever possible,' I said.

'Mmm . . . pleased to hear it,' she almost purred, and I suddenly had a feeling we were talking about two totally different things.

She liked to sleep naked from what I could see through the netting.

'Any idea why your name's really on that red folder?' she asked in an abrupt change of subject.

'Nope.' I let that sit there for a moment and then, 'CIA have apparently lost track of a female agent.'

'That's very careless of them.'

I nodded. 'Especially on top of those Globemasters going missing. Very careless indeed.'

'We'll have to see what we can sort out over breakfast,' she said with a yawn. 'We'll both think better with a clear head. Wake me if you want me to take over. I don't need a lot of sleep.'

Somewhere in one of the ornamental ponds a family of

frogs started their nocturnal chorus. It wasn't long before all the neighbourhood frogs joined in and we were in the middle of an amphibian symphony.

'Wayan thinks you're a witch.'

She didn't say anything.

'I didn't really believe in that stuff till I came to Bali.'

She nodded. 'It's a very mystical place. There's definitely a lot going on here.'

'So you *are* a witch?'

'I can neither confirm nor deny that possibility,' she laughed. 'Let's just say I'm a believer.'

'That must have gone down well with the shrinks at Langley.'

'My granny always said you should only ever tell people what it's necessary for them to know.'

Great, just what I needed, a room-mate with a gun, a CIA licence to kill and magical powers. As I leaned across to blow out the lamp I noticed she was looking at me. I knew that look. I'd tried it myself a number of times in the past, usually with limited success. Her dark hair cascaded over smooth shoulders and the lamplight through the netting cast a golden glow down one exposed thigh.

'You know,' she said, 'just for your information, a bit further down the track, under the right circumstances I'm not averse to a little recreational sex.'

'I am,' I said. 'I'm very old-fashioned. When I get into bed with a woman I want it to mean something.'

I saw her grinning at me from under the mosquito netting.

'And just for *your* information,' I said, 'I like to be wooed.'

As I blew out the lamp I could hear her laughing.

NINETEEN

It was around three in the morning when my dead friend Harry woke me up and saved my life. I'd been right about that last cup of coffee keeping me awake and when Grace's regular breathing indicated she wasn't going to sneak over and put the hard word on me or cast a spell, I took Harry's tape and the Walkman out onto the balcony.

Stretched out on the day bed, I watched the fireflies swooping in the moonlight and listened over and over to my carefully manufactured voice setting Harry up for a date with his last croissant. I must have played it back a dozen times before falling asleep. A couple of hours later I woke to Harry's voice and I remember feeling pleased that he'd been able to join us.

Realising where I was and what had happened jolted me wide awake. His voice was coming from the tape player but it wasn't the usual brief message. It took me a couple of seconds to figure out what was going on. While I'd slept, the tape had run to its end and the auto reverse had flipped over to side two. What had made Harry decide to leave a message on the other side of the tape? I struggled to make sense of what he was saying. I rewound the tape to the start and pressed 'Play'. It wasn't a very long recording but it was disturbing.

Harry had been about to give up on the Bitter Springs vetting as the usual waste of time when something had caught his eye. He said there were too many birthdays and mentioned the regular supply flights into the base. Then he said that there was something he needed to check out with Charlie. That was it. It appeared he'd decided to cover himself by leaving this recording as insurance. He finished with a promise to add more later as he sorted things out.

I rewound the tape to the start and was just about to press 'Play' again when I heard the truck. No-one drove this late in the mountains. After midnight the roads were empty. Then the truck stopped on the road above the hotel.

My hand over Grace's mouth was enough to wake her. She struggled momentarily and then I felt the muzzle of the Makarov against my temple. She must have had it under her pillow. I hoped she'd open her eyes and take a peek before she pulled the trigger. Luckily for me she did.

We were dressed and over the balcony into the darkness in seconds. Grace still had the pistol and I'd grabbed the empty ziplock bag and stuffed the cassette inside. The trail to the river was slippery and tricky enough in daylight but in the dark it was murderous. I had a small Mag-lite in my pocket but didn't dare use it so we just slipped and slid, trying to make as little noise as possible. When we stopped going downwards and were up to our waists in water I figured we'd reached the river. I doubt if it had taken us longer than ninety seconds from the sound of the truck stopping.

Now there was just silence. Whoever the people in the vehicle were, they were well trained. They had dismounted quietly and were probably spreading out to search the hotel. I was trying to figure out our next move when there was a *thump* and a small flash from the general vicinity of the hotel's driveway, followed by a lot of yelling.

'Claymore,' Grace said, and I nodded in agreement.

The M18A1 was developed for use in Korea in the early fifties but was made popular during the Vietnam War. Popular that is with anyone who wasn't standing in front of one when it went off. Take a curved steel plate, cover it with a pound and a half of C4 plastic explosive, add seven hundred steel balls, a trip-wire, or a long piece of thin electrical cable connecting a detonator at the C4 end to a soldier with a battery-operated triggering device at the other and you've got yourself a Claymore. It was like a giant shotgun and was the perfect perimeter defence weapon. What one was doing cluttering up Mungo's driveway was anyone's guess.

The blast of the antipersonnel mine and the cries of the wounded were followed by more yelling and the ripping sound of Kalashnikov assault rifles spraying the hotel. There was enough noise up top to cover the sound of us wading through the water as we headed downriver towards Ubud.

Thank God Mungo had sent Madé and Wayan home and kept his wife and kids away. But that was Mungo all over, always prepared. Just as the Boy Scouts motto suggested. I wondered what sort of merit badge you earned for wiring up a Claymore under the welcome mat.

We were dirty, wet, scratched and covered in mosquito bites when we climbed out of the river below the Tjampuhan Hotel just on daybreak. There was an arrow marked in yellow chalk on a rock jutting out of the water. That would be Mungo's work. After making our way carefully over the slippery, moss-covered rocks we climbed up some stone steps, passed a small shrine, went up some more steps and found ourselves in a cave, a very nice-smelling cave. I turned on my Mag-lite.

'Ali Baba's treasure cave?' Grace asked.

I swung the torch around. 'I think it's a day spa.'

'Thank goodness,' Grace said. 'I think I might have chipped a nail.'

A few dozen steps up from the spa is the hotel pool – spring-fed, icy cold and possibly the most beautiful in the world. The local prince had ordered it built for a glamorous Hollywood star in the thirties. We fell into it fully clothed and looking a lot less than glamorous. When I surfaced I saw Mungo was sitting on a sun lounge reading the *Jakarta Post*.

Grace and I clambered out of the pool and left a watery track across the terrace to the pile of towels stacked up on a table top.

'Coffee?' Mungo asked, holding up a pot.

We both nodded.

'I've ordered breakfast for you up on your balcony,' he said, handing me a room key along with my coffee. 'Just pound on the gong when you're ready. You two look like you could use a good hot shower.'

Mungo gave us each a small bottle of capsules. 'Antibiotics. Take two now and finish the full course.'

Grace gulped a couple of the pills down with her coffee.

'And there's antiseptic in the bathroom for those scratches, young lady,' Mungo continued. 'You really need to build up a bit of immunity before you can go splashing about in the local rivers like that.'

'Any idea who our visitors were?' I asked.

Mungo shook his head. 'Not a clue, dear boy, but I'll see what I can find out. You two stay here and keep your heads down till I get back.'

After we'd showered and cleaned up our bites and scratches I pounded on the bamboo gong on the balcony and ten minutes later there was a knock on the door: 'Room service'.

Grace moved into position, the Makarov cocked and ready as I opened the door and stepped clear. Two beaming waiters carried in trays holding spicy cheese and tomato omelettes, banana pancakes, freshly baked pastries, fruit salad and more coffee. '*Salamat pagi* . . . good morning,' they chorused.

'*Salamat pagi*,' Grace said graciously, concealing the pistol in the folds of her sarong.

For once we weren't all that hungry so we decided to take turns at getting some sleep but we were both much too keyed up. About eight o'clock Grace took off her sarong and climbed under my mosquito net.

'Enough wooing for you?' she asked.

'You think this is wise?' I couldn't actually believe I'd said it.

'Probably not,' she said, 'but assassins in the night put you in touch with your own mortality. And that makes me horny.'

She was right. I was feeling a bit toey even before I saw her naked. Apparently after disasters like earthquakes and hurricanes the first thing the survivors do is bonk themselves silly. It's a natural response to danger to ensure propagation of the species. And if a bloke had to do any propagating Grace wouldn't be too hard to take. But from the moment I'd set eyes on this woman people around me had been getting shot, run down or blown up.

'I know what happens to you when you get into bed with the US government,' I said.

'You're probably right on that,' she admitted, 'but actually I got into bed with you.'

She had a valid point but I still knew that somehow someone was going to wind up getting screwed.

TWENTY

The sex was great, but I'm a bloke so it always is. We're lucky that way. It was mid-morning now and Grace had disappeared in the direction of the spa. Sitting on the balcony in the warm sun, I went through all the options while sipping a cup of lukewarm leftover coffee poured from one of the insulated pots. From what I'd heard on Harry's tape it was now clear all the answers were back in Australia.

I turned on my mobile phone briefly to check for messages. There was only one, a short text from Julie: *'How's the satay?'* She was letting me know they knew I was in Bali but last night's little adventure had already clued me in. Getting off the island was now seriously urgent.

There was one knock on the door, a pause, then two more. It was the signal we'd agreed on but I picked up the pistol just in case. Grace let herself in. She looked amazing. There were frangipani blossoms in her hair and her skin was glowing.

'I just wanted a body scrub to get rid of the river germs,' she said, 'but they insisted on finishing me off with a yoghurt and curry wrap. I think I might smell a bit like something Madé could barbecue over a coconut husk fire and serve garnished with coriander.'

'I'd be willing to try a piece of that.'

Grace laughed. 'That's the trouble with you gourmets, you're never satisfied.'

The phone rang once and stopped. Then rang again, twice. That was Mungo's signal. There was a knock on the door two minutes later.

Mungo had some good news and a lot of bad news. On the good news side of things, the local rumour mill was saying that a couple answering our description had hired a fisherman to ferry them across to the nearby island of Lombok during the night. It was a simple diversion but it would buy us some time. I happened to know Mungo was very much part of the local rumour mill and it was most obliging of him to be so helpful after what had happened to his hotel. When I pointed this out he just shrugged.

'Nothing got set on fire,' he said, 'so the damage is minimal. Looks like those renovations are actually going to get done. The wife'll get her whole village in and a week from now you won't know anything ever happened.'

He was right about that. Mud brick, bamboo and thatch were easy to work with and in this climate and with the rich volcanic soil, the tropical gardens would instantly regenerate, masking any residual damage within days.

'Know who they were?' I asked.

He shook his head. 'Probably from off the island. They took their casualties with them and no-one's showed up at any of the local clinics so I guess they went back where they came from.'

'I think this has got Buzz Geiger's fingerprints all over it,' Grace said.

I nodded. 'That's what I was thinking. Lucky for us someone left a Claymore in the driveway.'

Mungo smiled. 'Wayan likes to put out his offerings for protection and I like to put out mine.'

'How long do you think the Lombok story will give us?' Grace asked.

Mungo shrugged. 'Not long, twenty-four to thirty-six hours at most. It's only a small island so they'll canvass it quickly. Then they'll backtrack this way. You should really start thinking about moving on, and fast. Got any ideas?'

'There's a couple with a yacht we've been sussing out. I know they're staying here and I think we might be able to hitch a ride with them.'

'Mid-forties? Fit? From Macau?'

I nodded.

'They're about to have lunch in the restaurant right now, dear boy. Lovely couple. We had a chat in the lobby.'

'Excellent,' Grace said, tossing me my pants. 'You didn't have much breakfast and I'm sure you've worked up an appetite by now.'

Mungo gave me a congratulatory glance, wished us a safe journey and headed back to his hotel to start the cleaning up.

'So you think you can talk them into taking us back to Australia?' Grace said.

I gave her sarong a tug. 'Maybe you should do it. You can be very persuasive.'

'Do you think we can trust them?' she asked, tightening the sarong back around herself.

'Well, we sure as hell know they can't trust *us*.'

Grace wanted to make sure she had all the marinade off her body so we took a quick shower together and behaved ourselves, which was much more her idea than mine.

We found them in the restaurant just as they were ordering.

'Hi again, mind if we join you?' Grace said in that easy-going American way.

Faith smiled. 'Why not?'

We settled into the table and the waiter brought menus.

'You two retired?' I asked.

Martin nodded. 'Sort of. I was a bank manager in a country town and Faith used to be a librarian.'

'And you bought yourselves a boat with your super payout?'

'Something like that,' Faith said. 'Enjoying the hotel then, Mike?' She put a lot of emphasis on the word 'Mike'.

'Yeah . . . it's great. Just what the doctor ordered.'

'Martin saw you arriving without your luggage this morning.'

'We were staying at Mungo's up the road,' I explained, 'but they've had to close for renovations.'

'So you took a leisurely moonlight swim down the river to get a room here?' Faith said with a smile. 'It's funny but I could have sworn I heard the gentle stutter of AK-47s going off up that way last night. That have anything to do with the need for renovations?'

I glanced down at the menu. Think fast, Alby. This woman doesn't miss a trick. They had *mee goreng*. This was Indonesia and everybody served *mee goreng*. I liked *mee goreng*. I could feel Faith's eyes burning into me, waiting for an explanation.

I put the menu down. 'We're in a serious situation here. I can't tell you the details but I'm not going to bullshit you either.'

'Good,' Faith said, 'saves me asking Mary Travers there for a rendition of "Puff the Magic Dragon".'

Grace laughed and I smiled and shook my head.

'Mary is actually Grace,' I said, 'and I'm actually Alby. She's a real Yank, though, I promise.'

'Alby Murdoch, right? The Markhor goat photo in the Hindu Kush.'

I looked at her. 'Have we met?'

'I saw you speak at a Nikon seminar a few years back. I like your work.'

'Thanks,' I said, relieved that I'd decided to tell the truth so far.

'You two sailing anywhere special?' I asked.

'Faith and I are just cruising about,' Martin said. 'We're tied up round at Padang Bai at the moment.'

'Martin was doing some cooking classes at the Honeymoon Guesthouse down the road,' Faith said.

'Did you learn the secret of their lime papaya pie?' I asked.

'You bet,' Faith said. 'He's got it down pat.'

'How is it that when you get more than two Australians at a table they start talking food?' Grace asked.

'It's because of the recent downturn in the residential property market,' I said. I thought it made sense and I noticed that Martin and Faith both laughed.

The food arrived. The *mee goreng* was delicious but it was hard to concentrate. A youngish American couple sat down at the next table and started a deep and meaningful at high volume. A woman with strong physical needs and a premature ejaculator are always going to be a bad match but why did they have to sit at the next table in a near-empty restaurant and talk so loudly? People were having lunch, for God's sake.

As we ate, Grace and I exchanged glances. She'd given me that Department of Justice story when we met but I was long past buying that and she hadn't disputed any of my CIA inferences. I was with D-E-D so it made perfect sense that we both knew what an AK sounded like. However, this retired librarian was a different kettle of fish, identifying the hammering of a Kalashnikov on full-auto, borne like a vapour on the still night air. And she knew who I was.

The premature ejaculator had finished his main course before his companion had even started to make a dent in hers. Seemed like he was a very quick eater, too. They left without having dessert.

'We've decided to head over to Manggis after lunch,' Martin said as he sipped his coffee. 'If you feel like a change of scenery you're welcome to join us.'

'What's in Manggis?' Grace asked.

'Great hotel called Alila. It's the next bay around from Padang Bai,' Faith said. 'We were going to check up on the boat on the way through, then spend a couple of days by the pool before stocking up at the local markets for the next leg of our trip.'

'What trip is that?' I asked.

'Just where the wind takes us,' Martin said. 'We're pretty flexible. We might be able to manage a detour, if it would help you out.'

'I did mention this was serious, didn't I?' I asked. 'I really don't want you two biting off more than you can chew.'

Faith laughed. 'Martin and I know pretty much what we can chew. We've been in a few tight corners and people have helped us out. Tell us whatever you can tell us on the trip over and we'll make up our minds when we get there. That suit you?'

Grace and I looked at each other and nodded at the same time. At the very least it would get us out of Ubud.

'Probably best if we're not seen leaving together,' Grace said. 'Maybe you could pick us up somewhere on the road.'

'Ary's Warung. Two o'clock?' Martin said.

Right. That was settled. Now I could concentrate on dessert. Mmm. Black rice pudding.

TWENTY-ONE

After lunch we walked up the road in the general direction of the Neka art gallery. When we were both certain we weren't being followed I hailed a bemo and we headed back down the hill past the Tjampuhan and over the bridge towards Ubud. Martin and Faith were loading their bags into the back of the rented Suzuki as we passed the hotel.

Right on two o'clock they picked us up outside Ary's Warung on the main drag in Ubud. Martin was driving. In an unspoken agreement Grace kept an eye on the road ahead while I watched for any sign of vehicles tailing us.

We drove east to Klung Kung and then took the rural backroads. As you head down towards the coastal plains the vegetation is not as lush as in the mountains but shimmering green rice terraces still dominate the landscape. Out here they grow the original and highly prized Balinese rice as well as the faster-ripening modern strains.

We passed schoolchildren dressed for the temple and processions of elegant families, the women wearing long-sleeved *kebayas* and tightly wrapped sarongs with colourful sashes around their waists and the men in loose shirts over their sarongs and hand-tied batik head scarves called *destar*.

Many of the women carried elaborate, towering offerings constructed from various fruit, rice cakes in different shapes and colours, and topped with flowers, which they balanced effortlessly on their heads. Offerings of this type meant they were heading off to celebrate the birthday of the temple so we were in luck to be passing by on such a special day.

We stopped briefly so Faith could take photographs of one group. Even the smallest of the children were dressed up in the same finery as their parents.

Further down the road we passed the temple and saw that it had been freshly cleaned and restored and that the celebrations had a carnival atmosphere with music, dancing, food stalls and cockfights.

Grace was just about used to the driving technique of the Balinese motorist by the time we reached the coast and she only yelped in terror twice before we got to Padang Bai.

In practical terms, for a vehicle to be roadworthy in Bali it must have a working horn, headlights that can be flashed at oncoming trucks on one-lane roads, and an accelerator pedal. Brakes are optional and generally only used when you arrive at your destination, and the flashing of headlights indicates that you are coming through, ready or not.

The Balinese combine a fatalistic approach to driving with the perfectly sensible belief that any accidents involving foreigners are always the fault of the foreigner. This is Bali and they live here, you are a foreigner and you don't live here. If you hadn't come to Bali then we wouldn't have had this accident so, logically, it must have been caused by you. It's a premise which really rattles the western concept of 'no fault' insurance.

Happily, and probably to Grace's disbelief, we reached Padang Bai without incident. Padang Bai is still a sleepy little town despite being a departure point for regular ferries to Lombok and less regular voyages to Surabaya in Java or Ujung Padang in Sulawesi. International luxury cruise liners also call occasionally but they have to anchor around the point towards Candi Dasa.

We turned left before the main ferry terminal and scooted down a side street then right and left again and we were on a sandy track running along a narrow strip of beach. There was a small shrine at the far end of the beach and a number of very simple thatch-roofed *warungs* built out onto the sand. Cheap accommodation of a variety of standards was on offer on the other side of the track. A dozen outboard-driven dive boats were riding at anchor close in and a white two-masted yacht was moored out in deeper water.

'There she is,' Martin said as he parked the Suzuki in close to a warung. 'We hired a local fishermen to stay on board for security. Why don't you two grab a drink while we go out and check her over.'

Grace chose the Kinky Bar for reasons unknown and we ordered a couple of Bintangs. Martin and Faith haggled with one of the boat owners and a couple of minutes later they were heading out to their yacht. Even in the shade of a tarpaulin it was hot on the beach and the sand was mostly broken-up coral which looked like it could rip our counterfeit Nikes to shreds.

Martin and Faith were back ten minutes later and they joined us at our table. As they ordered drinks Grace studied the moored yacht through some ancient binoculars she had borrowed from the owner of the warung.

'Beautiful lines,' she said. 'I like a ketch-rigged boat. It's a Cheoy Lee clipper, right?'

'On the money,' Faith said. 'You sail?'

Grace nodded and I reached for the binoculars. The yacht was semi stern-on to us and there was a small zodiac tied to the rail. The binoculars' optics were fuzzy with tropical fungus but behind the inflatable boat I could just make out the name of the yacht.

'*Belle Chance*,' I read out loud. 'Good name.'

Martin nodded. 'We like it.'

'She okay as a two-hander?' Grace asked.

Faith shrugged. 'It can get a bit hectic in heavy weather.'

'We caught the edge of a typhoon off Hong Kong when

we were doing a shakedown,' Martin said, 'and we found out exactly how much we had to learn. And we learned it pretty fast.'

'How does she handle under sail?' Grace asked.

'She's best on a reach,' Faith replied, 'then you can get up some decent speed. Upwind and downwind she's a bit of a barge but we didn't buy her for pace. We're all about style and comfort.'

This seafaring chatter was interesting but we really needed to sort out our chances of a ride back to Oz. On the drive to Padang Bai I'd told Martin and Faith that Grace was a journalist with *Time* magazine and we'd been working on a story about illegal forest-clearing in Tanjung Puting National Park in central Kalimantan that was threatening the habitat of the orangutans. Logging these protected forests was a multi-million-dollar business and we'd crossed the wrong people, people with connections in high places, people without scruples. People who were now after us. We couldn't leave the country openly as we'd heard we were on watch lists all over Asia and whoever wanted us out of the way was closing in fast. I almost believed it myself by the time I got to the end of the tale.

Martin and Faith seemed unfazed by the story. But, hey, the woman knew the sound of an AK in the night so I had a feeling not much would faze her.

'You two get anywhere on the subject of a couple of stowaways heading south?' I asked.

'We might be up for a leisurely cruise down the coast in the general direction of Broome if that's any help,' Martin said.

'We can run you ashore in the rubber duckie,' Faith added, 'but we'd prefer not to put into any major ports.'

Hmm, I wonder why that was. Still, if they were willing to take a chance on us I wasn't about to go digging around in their private affairs. They didn't seem like drug runners or arms smugglers so what did I care? 'Perfect,' I said. 'When do we leave?'

'How about we do this,' Faith said. 'We'll drop you off near the entrance to the Alila. You guys check in for a week and look like you're getting comfortable. Martin and I will stock up on provisions at the markets in Karangasem and head back to the yacht. If you wander out for a romantic late-night moonlit stroll on the beach around two-ish one of us will be waiting in the zodiac.'

My respect for librarians was growing by the minute. I could see that Grace was impressed too.

'You should pay for the week up-front,' Martin said. 'You got enough cash?'

I nodded.

'Good. The economy might be picking up but everyone's been doing it tough enough on this island without you stiffing them on the hotel bill.'

I decided I might have to consider changing my opinion of bank managers as well.

TWENTY-TWO

I hadn't been to this part of the island for some time but I recognised the road where they dropped us off. A few years back Manggis was just a place that you went through five minutes before you got to Candi Dasa. The road back then was simply a track leading to a coconut grove. Beyond the grove was a tranquil, stony beach, a jumble of the local sail-powered, brightly painted outrigger fishing boats called *jukungs*, and some tumbledown shacks occupied by fishermen and their families. But that was then. And 'then' in Bali is never the same as now.

Now a sign welcomed us to the Alila and several stylish, low-rise buildings sat amidst the coconut palms, nestling next to the beach with clear views out across the straits to Nusa Penida and back to a cloud-shrouded Mount Agung. I liked the look of the Alila. It was very much in harmony with its natural surroundings. The thatch-roofed lobby was filled with the perfume from great pots of white cempaka flowers and I looked across at the empty pool and the nearly empty restaurant and knew we wouldn't have to beg for a room. Business might have been picking up down south but on this part of the island it was a buyer's market.

I took the first rate they offered us and booked for the week. We got a ground-floor room in the block nearest to the beach. It would make for an easy stroll off the open terrace and across the lawn to where I could hear the waves breaking. In simpler times it was the kind of place I could happily spend a few weeks, settling into the rhythm of the locals, photographing the comings and goings of the fishermen and the villagers working the fields.

Dinner in the restaurant looked promising, going by the interesting menu and the news that they had a new Balinese chef in the kitchen. I hoped Martin had picked up a few pointers in his cooking courses because we had a long voyage ahead of us. We ordered more than we could eat – my fault as usual.

As we shared a salad of Balinese black beans, roasted green papaya, cucumber and grated coconut, Grace and I tried to put together the pieces that connected Harry's death with the missing Globemasters.

The giant transport planes made regular supply flights to US bases around the world: England, Germany, Korea, Turkey – lots of places, including Australia, where they landed at Larunga, originally a World War II emergency strip. It had been upgraded to handle the RAAF's Mirage fighters during the sixties. In 1980, when the US spy station was sited some forty-five k's away at Bitter Springs, an all-weather road was put in and the strip was upgraded to handle the Globemasters.

During construction of the base the big freighters were landing at the rate of four or five a day for six months. A constant shuttle of trucks ran twenty-four hours a day, moving equipment and supplies. Since the base's opening in 1982 there had been two flights a month with replacements, fuel and food for the three hundred US personnel. It was a hardship posting for the Americans. No families, but all the frozen pizza you could eat.

We agreed that Bitter Springs definitely held the missing pieces to the puzzle but getting in to find out what they were was going to be a major problem. Security at the Springs was very good. I'd photographed the base once as part of a diversionary exercise. Long-lens shots from six miles out, which is as close as I could get even with my security clearance. The images were electronically altered to conceal most major features, extra grain and a little camera shake were added and the pictures were leaked through a West German magazine. Gordon's rationale was that if people thought they could see shots of the base it would keep them from going out trying to take their own. I was only half a kilometre past the DO NOT PROCEED PAST THIS POINT sign when a base security helicopter started blowing sand into my cameras.

After dinner Grace headed back to the room and I

wandered down to the water. There was sand higher up but at the waterline it was a black pebble beach. The stones, rounded and smoothed by the action of the waves, rattled constantly as the sea water washed in over them and retreated. A dozen of the local fishermen had been trying for one last catch. The fishing boats were pulled up above the tide line on coconut-log rollers and men were standing waist deep in the water, gradually closing, hand over hand, a wide circle made up of a fine net. They eventually wrestled the net ashore but there wasn't much worth keeping. The light on the beach was very flat now but early in the morning or late in the afternoon it would be magic and I made a mental note to come back one day to try to capture this scene on film.

I went back to our room and listened to Harry's tape a few more times out on the terrace. The bit about the birthdays still didn't make any sense but he'd said that he was going to check something out with Charlie. That had to be Charles Somersby, a computer boffin with the Department of Defence until he'd retired. He and Harry did some liaison work in Canberra and had stayed in touch after Somersby moved to Byron Bay. Somersby might have some answers.

I glanced into the room. Grace had woken up and she was looking back. She smiled.

'You should close those shutters on the way over here,' she said.

The sex that morning had not been so much recreational as therapeutic. We'd both been stressed and exhausted. Grace didn't look stressed or exhausted now. In fact she looked positively dangerous. I closed the shutters to the balcony.

'I should warn you I'm having a bit of performance anxiety after listening to that couple at the next table at lunch,' I said. 'I wouldn't want to develop a reputation at the CIA as a dud bash.'

She looked at me. 'A what?' she asked. Again she didn't dispute the CIA link.

'A dud bash is a less-than-stellar sexual performer,' I explained.

She shook her head. 'Who said that thing about "two peoples separated by a common language"?'

I shrugged. I was busy taking off my sarong.

'Anyway,' she said, 'you don't have to worry. I'm not into holding up scorecards.'

Five minutes later I discovered that she had incredibly sensitive nipples. Five minutes after that we discovered that I did too.

When I woke up it was dark outside. I could hear Grace in the shower and when I rolled over I found a small piece of paper on the pillow. There was a single number on it. She'd given me a nine. I smiled. Then I frowned and looked at the paper again, more carefully. Maybe it was a six.

TWENTY-THREE

Rhythmic chanting drew us to a spot on the grass near the hotel's small temple. The local villagers were putting on a *Kechak* and there was a coconut-husk fire burning, the smoke mixing in the warm night air with the smell of the sea and the sweet aroma of frangipani.

It was a big troupe, since many of the villagers who had left to work in the hospitality trade across the island had now been forced to return home. I like the *Kechak*, even if it is more of a tourist performance than an actual ritual dance. The rhythmic swaying and chanting of over a hundred bare-chested men in black-and-white chequered sarongs sitting in a huge circle in the firelight as a backdrop to the story of brave Prince Rama, his main squeeze the gorgeous spunk Sita, and their offsider Hanuman the white monkey, always does it for me. Grace looked like she got into it too. At the end they threw in a bit of a trance dance with some firewalking and the evening finished with flaming coconut husks being kicked all over the lawn.

The smell of smoke was still lingering hours later when we stepped quietly out onto the terrace and crossed the grass to the path to the ocean. There was a three-quarter moon and everything was still except for the splash of the waves and the rattling of the black stones on the beach as the water ran back out to sea. A scrawny yellow dog sleeping on the beach opened one eye, checked us out and then went back to sleep after deciding we probably weren't worth the energy it would take to rustle up a bark.

I was trying to decide if we should walk east or west along the beach when the black inflatable hull of the zodiac ran up on the stones beside me. First of all I thought it was a bit of good luck and then I saw the night-vision goggles on Martin's head. A slightly built Balinese man was standing next to him.

'This is Nyoman, our security guard. I brought him along to make sure I found the right spot. He lives just up the beach.'

Nyoman smiled and jumped effortlessly out of the zodiac onto the pebbles. We pushed the boat around and a minute later the almost silent electric outboard motor was taking us back to sea with a soft '*Salamat jalan*' from Nyoman carried across the waves.

My awkward scrambling into the rubber boat was made more embarrassing by Grace's neat flip over the side after we'd turned it around. I'd seen that same move once before in a classified film on how the US Navy trained its elite SEAL commandos.

In less than ten minutes we were aboard the *Belle Chance* with the zodiac tied off, the sails set and a course charted down through the Lombok Strait and then south to Broome. Faith was at the wheel and Grace and Martin worked the sails under her directions. I found a bottle of rum in a well-equipped little bar and had a tot. It was the most nautical thing I could find to do.

As dawn broke we picked up a steady breeze and a school of dolphins joined us for a while. The more adventurous played at surfing in our bow wave as we slipped down the waterway separating Bali and Lombok. We could make out the land masses of both islands and the four of us sat quietly in the stern of the boat enjoying the wind in our faces.

'Historic bit of water, this,' I said. 'Z Force sailed up this way, heading for Singapore in the *Krait*.'

'In a crate?' Grace asked.

'K-R-A-I-T. It's a small and very deadly snake,' I explained. 'It's the name they gave to a captured Japanese fishing boat that a bunch of Aussie and Brit commandos sailed from Australia to Singapore in 1943 – Operation Jaywick it was called. The *Krait*'s original name was the *Kofuku Maru* so anything would have been an improvement.'

Grace looked towards Lombok and then back across in the direction of Bali. 'Bit of a tight squeeze.'

'The Japanese army was on either side,' I said, 'and their navy was stooging around on the wet bit, so Z Force sailed through at night with the lights off and everything crossed.'

'What was so interesting in Singapore?' Grace asked.

'Docks full of enemy shipping,' Faith said, 'especially tankers. Six of the Z Force blokes paddled in at night in three folding canoes and put limpet mines on anything they could reach. They got away with it and sailed back to Australia but were caught when they tried to do it again. Not a happy ending.'

We sailed on in silence for a long while.

'And we're also zooming down the Wallace Line,' Faith said eventually.

Martin looked at her and smiled. 'I'll bite,' he said.

'This strait is only about fifteen miles wide but on the Lombok side over there to the east the flora and fauna are totally different to what you find to the west on Bali and beyond.'

'That's wild,' Grace said.

'Alfred Russel Wallace was a pretty sad dude,' Faith continued. 'You could make a fairly persuasive argument that he discovered the theory of evolution rather than Darwin. Poor bugger just didn't know how to parlay it into international fame.'

'Jesus, Faith,' I said, 'is there anything you don't know?'

'Occasionally, when to shut up,' she said.

'Faith's got a photographic memory,' Martin said with a grin. 'Never forgets a face or a fact. Now who's up for breakfast?'

Everyone nodded. Martin stood up and Faith gave him a friendly slap on the butt as he made his way below deck.

'Feel comfortable taking the wheel, Grace?' Faith asked, glancing up at the sky.

Grace nodded.

'I'll go and give Martin a hand in the galley, then.'

I stood up. 'Why don't you take it easy, I'll be the kitchen hand, since I'm not much good at any of the yachtie stuff.'

'Deal,' Faith agreed. 'But I'll go and clean up a bit and sort out your accommodation.'

There was a framed photograph on the galley wall of Faith, Martin and two men, all smiling for the camera. They were on a rooftop terrace garden, and there was a familiar skyline visible in the background. At first glance I thought it was Lisbon, then I realised it was Macau. One of the blokes, who looked Vietnamese, was holding a beagle in his arms. I recognised both of the men.

'Isn't that Jack Stark?' I said.

Startled, Martin looked up from the chopping board and nodded.

Stark, a decorated Vietnam vet, apparently went crazy a

few years after the war and holed up in a booby-trapped bunker on a mountain in Far North Queensland. Rumour had it he was paranoid, convinced that the world was controlled by a giant conspiracy of corrupt politicians and big business.

But Mungo had always said there was a lot more to Stark's story than met the eye and I was curious.

'How'd you know the Mad Major?' I asked.

Martin, now busily whisking eggs in a large bowl, looked up again. 'We were in high school together.'

'This doesn't look like a high-school photo.'

'I caught up with him a while back.'

'Before the accident?'

Martin stared at me.

'Rumour was he blew himself up with his chemistry set doing things he shouldn't have been doing.'

'I heard that rumour.'

I'd heard other rumours too and some of them suggested Jack Stark wasn't all that dead. 'I thought he was supposed to be a bit of a nutter. He doesn't look too crazy there.'

Martin carefully poured the whisked eggs into a pan. 'One of the sanest men I've ever met. Good man to have in your corner.'

'I'd have to second that. Stark and that Vietnamese bloke pulled me out from underneath a bar brawl in Bangkok in '79.'

'Well, bugger me,' Martin smiled. 'What a coincidence. Small world, eh?'

'Sure is.' And I hoped it *was* just a coincidence. I liked this Martin bloke but a connection to Jack Stark was a surprising complication.

TWENTY-FOUR

After breakfast Faith gave Grace a quick familiarisation on the quirks of the *Belle Chance* and then disappeared below deck. She reappeared an hour later with a dozen fresh black-and-white photographic prints still dripping with water. They were shots she'd taken at the Barong dance in Ubud and they were very good. The quality of her printing was excellent too.

'Great prints,' I said. 'You've held a lot of shadow detail.'

'Thanks,' she said with a smile. 'But they're just work prints. When I get back into a proper darkroom I'll be able to make them really sing.'

Good black-and-white printing is a dying art. Good black-and-white printing on a forty-two-foot yacht under sail in the Lombok Strait is a total mystery, so I had to ask.

Faith took me below to show me the smallest darkroom I'd ever seen. Tucked neatly into a small alcove beside the shower cubicle, the tiny work space was well planned and beautifully built. The secret was a vertical print-processing tank which took up less room than one of the three developing trays you would usually need.

'Must eat into your fresh-water supply,' I said.

Faith shook her head. 'I use sea water to wash the prints.'

'That works?' I asked.

'You bet. After World War II the US Navy's photographic section at Pearl Harbor noticed that pictures taken and processed at sea on its warships were lasting longer than the ones processed normally on land. Out at sea they were washed in pure salt water and they got a more archival result. Works for me too.'

Martin called from up top about having to tack or jib or some other nautical falderal so Faith excused herself and raced up the narrow steps to the deck. I inspected the tiny darkroom and, being the suspicious type, gave the backs of a couple of the storage cupboards a bit of a nudge. You get an eye for a shallow cupboard fitted into a space where a deep one would easily go. One popped open on recessed hinges to reveal a slim hiding place and some oilskin-wrapped packages sitting in a neat set of custom-made pigeonholes. The shapes of the bundles and the smell of gun oil was enough but I unwrapped one anyway, to be sure. Just what every well-equipped ocean-going darkroom needs: a Heckler and Koch MP5 submachine gun with a full magazine. From the shapes of the other packages it looked like another SMG, some kind of assault rifle and a couple of pistols. These days you'd be crazy to sail through Asian waters without some kind of protection but this little arsenal was seriously heavy-duty. I made a quick mental note not to make any disparaging remarks about Martin's cooking or Faith's photographic skills.

Just as I closed the concealed door, Grace called down through the companionway. 'We need you on deck Alby, right now.'

Her voice was calm but the 'right now' had that same kind of urgency that pilots recognise when air traffic controllers request that they descend to ten thousand feet IMMEDIATELY. Before the end of the last syllable they have their 747's nose down and engines at full throttle, hoping to get out of the way of whatever the hell's coming at them.

I was on deck in seconds. Faith was at the wheel and Grace pointed towards a white splashing in the water off the stern to starboard. She handed me a large pair of binoculars. They were Zeiss with excellent optics, and when I got the image clearly focused I really didn't like what I could see.

'Trouble?' Martin asked. He sounded surprisingly calm.

'Big trouble,' I said.

I glanced at the sun and then at my watch. It was just after eleven. So much for my gran's theory that the boogymen only come for you in the night-time.

The Bugis, who gave the world the term 'Boogyman', originated in the south-western part of the island of Sulawesi and had a long history as shipbuilders, sailors, merchants, slavers, adventurers, warriors, and pirates; most especially pirates. With a well-deserved reputation for savagery, the Bugis were the most feared of the old-time pirates of the Java Sea, hunting down their prey in packs in ships fitted with dragon-shaped cast-bronze bow rammers.

I couldn't really make out whether the six or seven dark-skinned men in sarongs and tattered shirts on the speedboat were actually Bugis, but I knew the heavy machine gun mounted on the bow would do a lot more damage than any bronze rammer. They were closing fast and I also knew we had better get some sort of a plan into action or we'd be in real trouble. At most we had five minutes. I focused the binoculars on a string of round white balls linked over the front of the speedboat but with the bowspray and bounce I couldn't quite make out what they were.

'Almost certainly pirates,' I said, handing the binoculars back to Grace.

'Pirates,' she said. 'You're kidding, right?'

''Fraid not,' Martin said.

'Nope,' I said. 'Piracy on the high seas is big business these days. They'll attack and board any commercial vessel that looks tempting and steal the cargo before selling or sinking the ship.'

'What happens to the crew?' Grace asked.

'Usually nothing very pleasant,' I said. This was an understatement. 'Think we can outrun them, Faith?'

She shook her head. 'Not a chance. These older clippers are cruisers, not racers. Even with the engine cranked right up.'

'I make it seven onboard,' Grace said, putting the binoculars on the deck. 'What do you think they want?'

'The yacht, probably,' I said. 'They'd repaint and rename her and sell her on with forged papers. Or they could be after us. Either way we've got a fight on our hands.'

'This isn't going to be much good against that fifty on their bow,' Grace said as she pulled out the Makarov.

'We've got weapons onboard,' Faith said.

'I know,' I said. Grace and Martin and Faith all looked at me. 'But those MP5s are only good for close in and by the time their boat's in range we'll be dead in the water, literally.'

'MP5s are better than nothing but we need some kind of stand-off weapon to keep them at a distance,' Grace said. 'Got anything heavier?'

Martin jumped down the companionway and returned with the two MP5s and the longer oilskin-wrapped weapon. He handed me the package and I handed it on to Grace since she was the one rated 'marksman'. She knelt down to unwrap it, which was a smart move in case they also had binoculars on the speedboat.

'Whoa,' she said, 'an oldie but a goodie. This'll do the job.'

It was a Rock Island Arsenal M21 tactical rifle: a Vietnam-era conversion of the most accurate of the superseded M14 military-issue rifles made by fitting an adjustable ranging telescopic sight and a bipod. They were well past their use-by date but this particular weapon looked to be in almost mint condition.

'A PSG1 would be better,' I said. The H and K Police Precision Rifle with its 6 × 42 Hensoldt telescopic sight is the pre-eminent marksman's weapon, delivering surgically accurate multiple shots to distant targets.

Grace shook her head. 'Magazine capacity's our edge with this one.'

The old M21 was heavy but it was semi-automatic like the PSG1 and held ten 7.62mm rounds in the magazine as opposed to the PSG1's five. Grace was right: for what was probably coming up, the M21 was perfect. Even the traditional bolt-action sniper rifle would have been way too slow to do what had to be done. The person who set up the darkroom on this boat knew all about darkrooms and whoever chose the weaponry had a good idea of what they were doing as well.

Grace checked the magazines and the action on the rifle before quickly scanning the deck for a place to set up.

'Should we heave to?' Faith asked.

Grace gave a negative shake of her head. 'Keep her steady as she goes, and as stable as possible. Once we start shooting I've got to finish it as fast as I can.'

She glanced up at me and spoke softly. 'These clippers are moulded fibreglass and they've got about nine thousand pounds of cast-iron ballast hanging off the bottom of the hull. If we take even half a dozen hits below the waterline from that fifty cal she'll sink like a stone.'

Once the crew of the speedboat knew we were armed they could just stand off and cut us to pieces with their machine gun. They were closing fast now and Grace took up a position lying low on the deck, resting the bipod on the cabin roof. I kept moving back and forward in front of her to interrupt their view.

There was a *thump* from the speedboat and then a plume of water exploded upwards off our port side. Martin and Faith looked at me.

'Mortar,' I yelled. 'Not very accurate at sea but it's usually enough to scare the crews on freighters and oil tankers into surrendering. It'd be a bloody miracle if they could hit a moving target our size and they'll want the boat in one piece.'

What I didn't say was that if they hit us, even unintentionally, it'd be a bloody miracle if there were any pieces left bigger than a matchstick.

The speedboat was drawing level with us now, and was about three hundred metres to starboard.

'What should I do?' Martin asked.

'Load the MP5s, then stay calm and look confused,' I said. 'If they want the yacht to sell they'll try to avoid shooting it full of holes. But when Grace opens up all bets are off.'

'I don't want to seem like a namby-pamby,' Faith yelled, 'but are we overreacting a bit? Opening fire on them without any warning, I mean.'

She had a point, but since they'd already put the equivalent of a shot across our bow with the mortar, I'd say we were justified. I picked up the binoculars again. One of the pirates was sharpening a large machete on a whetstone and now that the boat was closer and had slowed a little, I realised what the round white objects on the bow were. Human skulls.

'Don't worry about the niceties any more, Faith,' I yelled. 'Believe me, these guys have got it coming.'

'I'm as ready as I'll ever be,' Grace said. 'Just hold her as steady as you can, Faith, and keep your head down.'

'Roger that,' Faith said.

'MP5s loaded and cocked?' I asked Martin.

He gave me the thumbs-up.

Grim as things were, I still had to smile. These two really were an interesting couple.

'When Grace starts shooting we'll open up with the sub-guns on full auto and give them all we've got. It's just a distraction at this range but it'll keep their attention off Grace.'

The speedboat was now level with us and beginning to draw ahead, which I knew would be better from Grace's point of view. Someone started yelling at us through a megaphone and the pirates posed dramatically with AK-47s and shotguns on their hips in a manner that was supposed to frighten us into submission. They would have had us pegged as just a bunch of yuppie yachties who'd give up without a fight. The gunner on the fifty-calibre in the bow wasn't even aiming his weapon our way.

'Set,' Grace said loudly. Then, 'Clear my shot.'

I moved clumsily towards the rear of the yacht and put my hands up in a rather dramatic show of surrender. The pirates started laughing and allowed their boat to drift in closer to us. They probably laughed even louder when I tripped and fell headfirst into the cockpit. They stopped laughing when Martin and I sat up with the MP5s and started firing. Grace's first shot punched the guy behind the fifty-calibre right out of the boat.

The rest of the crew looked blankly at the empty spot where the gunner had been. Two more were down before they realised what was happening and two more after that before they'd even fired a single shot in our direction. One of the pirates opened up with his AK while the last remaining crewman scrambled forward towards the heavy machine gun. Martin and I ducked below the gunwale to change magazines, though I knew the Cheoy Lee's fibreglass hull wasn't going to stop any bullets, even at this range.

When I peeked up again the guy on the fifty was pulling back the cocking lever and then one of Grace's bullets smacked into the chest of the guy firing the AK and he went down into the boat with his finger locked on the trigger.

He must have emptied most of his magazine into the fuel

tanks because without warning the speedboat exploded in a massive fireball.

The blazing wreck slowed and then stopped and was quickly far behind us, the black smoke from the fire smudging the clear blue sky. Martin and Faith were sitting in the cockpit trying to catch their breath. They were both very pale.

I put the MP5s to safe and began throwing the empty brass shell casings over the side. Grace was sitting on the roof of the cabin with her head between her knees. I could make out nine empty shell casings beside her. Six hits and three misses or three of the pirates got two bullets each. My money was on the second scenario.

I knew enough to leave her alone for a while. Martin and I were just spraying bullets while she was looking through the high-power scope and methodically working out who she was going to kill and in what order. No amount of training and conditioning can ever make that into just a job. There was a bottle of excellent Scotch in the bar and I grabbed it and took a swig. I was trying very hard not to embarrass myself by being the first on board to lose their breakfast over the side.

Martin and Faith each took a drink and after a few minutes I walked carefully across the deck and offered the bottle to Grace. She looked up and shook her head. Her eyes were still that amazing grey but right now they were full of pain.

'Inventive distraction,' she said quietly, 'pretending to fall over your feet into the cockpit.'

I nodded and smiled. 'In my youth I was known for my gymnastic prowess.'

'How's your swimming?' she asked.

'Okay, I guess,' I answered, confused. 'Why?'

'Because you might want to do up that shoelace. Next time you trip on it you're liable to go straight over the goddamn side.'

TWENTY-FIVE

We settled into a routine fairly quickly. Because they had been sailing two-handed, Martin and Faith's usual practice had been to anchor inshore for the night, which was easy to do when you're island-hopping down the Indonesian archipelago. Now that we had a lot of open water to cross we did alternate four-hour shifts, Martin and Faith together and then Grace at the helm with me wandering around and doing as I was told. Grace had crewed on ocean racers off Rhode Island when she was in college and was totally at home at the wheel.

The yacht was beautifully restored and it was obvious they'd spent a lot of money on the rebuild and refit. Solar panels and a couple of small wind-driven turbines generated constant power for the fridge and freezer, and the galley had been designed by somebody who really knew how to cook. You had to wonder exactly what sort of superannuation payouts rural bank managers and librarians were pulling down these days.

When they weren't sailing the boat, Martin and Faith spent a lot of time sleeping, or at least in their cabin at the pointy end. Grace let me steer one afternoon while she went forward to untangle a sheet. She came back with a smile on her face.

'Those two have quite an enthusiastic love-life for people their age,' she said.

'Watch yourself, girlie,' I said, 'I'm almost people their age.'

Grace held up her hands. 'Just commenting,' she said, 'not complaining.'

The compact cabin we shared was aft, but located too damn close to the wheel for comfort. The proximity to the skipper and first mate was a bit inhibiting and the events with the pirates and the M21 were still very fresh. Even though what Grace had to do was totally justified, it wasn't something you got over in a hurry. Mostly she just wanted to be held and woken gently out of the nightmares. This was okay by me since I'd been there, and to tell the truth, she'd come pretty damn close to giving me a coronary during our interlude at Manggis. Besides, recreational sex is like recreational tennis: after a couple of sets it's great to sit back under an umbrella with a gin and tonic and just relax.

I liked Grace a lot but in this business it doesn't help to get too attached. For one thing you can never be sure exactly who you're getting attached to. Grace's cover story was basically all I knew about her. Neither of us had opened up much to the other. There were lots of things happening that didn't make sense and too many people in my orbit seemed to be either shooting at me or getting shot. I was just as happy to play my cards close to my chest as well.

So we settled into a routine of cooking and eating, sleeping and eating, and sailing and eating. The cooking was left to me and Martin as neither Grace nor Faith was at home in the kitchen. However, when it came to consuming the results of our labour they were in a league of their own.

Martin insisted on doing the breakfasts, which were always spectacular, and he had a stock of a homemade tomato and chilli relish that was out of this world.

By the time we made the coastline just north of Broome I was feeling refreshed, rested and relaxed. A longish ocean voyage, good food, laid-back company and not getting shot at for a couple of days can make quite an improvement in your disposition.

My head was clear now and I was champing at the bit to get back on home soil and track down Charles Somersby in Byron Bay. I was sure that he would have some of the answers to the riddle I was desperately trying to unravel about Harry, birthdays and Bitter Springs.

It was late afternoon and Faith suggested we drift down

with the current overnight and take a short ride ashore in the zodiac just before dawn. Since she'd managed to navigate us across a lot of open ocean right to the spot she promised, I was happy to leave the decision to her. When she gave Grace a brief run-down of Broome's history as a pearling port it was hard to stop the girl jumping over the side in search of an elegant pair of matching earrings.

Martin suggested something special for dinner in honour of our return home. We spotted a marker buoy just after dusk and he hauled up a craypot and selected four very tasty-looking lobsters. I thought it was a little mean but then he replaced the feisty crustaceans with a new hundred-dollar note sealed in an empty beer bottle. There would be a very mystified cray fisherman the next time that particular pot was checked.

I'd become familiar with the galley over the past few days but I still found things that were intriguing. There was a freezer as well as a refrigerator but also a range of double clay pots tucked under a workbench. The inner and outer pots were separated by a layer of wet sand. When covered with a damp hessian cloth the system had managed to keep a lot of the more robust fruits and vegetables they'd stocked up on in Karangasem in good shape.

Martin checked over the contents of his larder. 'How does black-pepper lobster with a potato and lychee salad sound?'

It sounded good to me, I must admit. I checked the front of my shirt to make sure I wasn't drooling.

'I'll whack a couple of those Bali whites on ice,' Martin went on, 'and if it doesn't work we won't give a rat's anyway.'

The meal was spectacular, eaten under the stars on the rear deck of the *Belle Chance*.

Martin raised his glass. 'Here's to you two for saving our lives and our boat.'

We all joined in the toast. 'And to you two for rescuing us from the wrath of those Kalimantan loggers and getting us back to Australian shores,' I said.

Faith took a sip of her wine. 'Yes, those pesky loggers. After Mike and Mary, weren't they?'

I shot a glance at Grace. 'What do you mean?'

'Well, just like I didn't believe you were Mike and Mary I didn't buy the line about the outraged loggers either,' Faith said.

'Why not?'

'The area you were talking about was fully cleared 18 months ago. That story ran in *Time* around then with your name credited as the photographer.'

'Oh.' Damn, this woman was good. I'd just grabbed for some past assignment that would logically place us in Indonesia and she'd seen right through it.

Martin smiled. 'She's got one of those memories. I warned you.'

'Yep, I guess you did,' I said.

'Who could forget that close-up of the orphaned baby orangutan's eyes?' Faith said. 'It made me cry.'

'Why did you agree to help us then if you didn't buy our story?'

'Your name came up once when I was talking to Jack Stark and saying how much I admired your work. He reckoned that some of the photographers at WORLDPIX were actually undercover agents for an ultra-secret intelligence agency.'

'And he'd know?'

Faith smiled. 'I reckon he would.'

I held her eye for a long moment.

'Anyway,' she went on, 'we knew you were spinning us a line but since that gunfire up the hill in Ubud was the real thing we figured you might have been in real trouble. Martin and I know that feeling.'

Martin nodded. 'And since sailing about can get a bit monotonous after a while we were up for a little diversion. Could have done without the pirates though.'

'Lucky for us you had that arsenal aboard,' Grace said.

'You'd be crazy to cruise these waters without some kind of protection,' Martin said.

'Most people make do with a shotgun and maybe a couple of Ruger Mini-14s,' I said. 'For a supposedly retired bank manager and librarian you two are extremely well kitted out.'

Martin looked up from his lobster. 'Supposedly?'

It was my turn to be blunt. 'You didn't buy a boat like this with an early super payout from the Commonwealth Bank.'

'No, it was Austwide Sansho, actually.' Martin smiled.

Faith laughed a hearty, throaty laugh. 'And it wasn't a super payout. He was retrenched.'

'Must have been a hefty severance cheque?' Grace said.

Faith laughed again, then turned to Martin. 'Sorry, Marty. They did save our lives. We should tell them the story.'

'Okay.' Martin took a sip of his wine. 'I woke up one morning and suddenly I was fifty, I was overweight and unfit, my wife was playing around on me, the step kids hated my guts, I was being retrenched after thirty years with the bank, and every bastard had forgotten my birthday. I seriously thought about ending it all.'

I sympathised. 'Everyone's had at least one day like that, mate!'

'*I* haven't!' Grace said.

'Not yet,' I said. 'Give it another twenty years.'

Martin laughed and continued, 'Anyway, on my last morning a million bucks in cash arrived at my branch – final payroll for the local abattoir that was closing down. Dunno how it happened exactly but I picked up a pistol and knocked over my own bank.'

Grace spluttered into her wine. 'You're kidding?'

Faith didn't miss a beat. 'He's not.'

'What, you just robbed your own bank and went on the lam?' Grace asked.

Martin shrugged. 'Basically . . . yes.'

Grace turned to Faith. 'But you're not the wife who was playing around on him?'

'Good lord, no!' Faith said.

'So how did you two hook up?' I said.

'I had a brush with cancer, which inspired me to ditch an unhappy marriage and hit the road on a 500cc Ducati. Got into a spot of bother with a homicidal bikie and Marty here – bank manager on the lam – came to my rescue.' She gave Martin a warm look. 'Been together ever since.'

Fuck me drunk! I know everyone has a story but these two had enough for a whole bloody book. But then again, who would believe it?

We had finished off the second bottle of white and then moved on to a vintage port Martin pulled out of a cupboard.

I raised my glass. 'To the Bonnie and Clyde of the baby-boomer generation.'

Grace was fascinated. 'How come you guys didn't get caught?'

Martin put down his glass. 'Long story. But suffice to say we managed to get to Jack's place and he was good enough to put us up and help us get out of the country.'

'Sounds like this Stark guy was pretty well connected,' Grace said.

'Stark's place was a fortified bunker on a hilltop in Queensland,' I said. 'He was supposed to be a bit of a psycho but rumour had it he was actually working for the CIA at one stage.'

'Imagine that,' Grace smiled, 'crazies working for the CIA. Hard to believe.'

That got a laugh.

'And Stark managed to get you out of the country,' I said to Faith, 'before he was blown up in his mountain retreat?'

Faith chose her words carefully. 'Before it blew up. Yes.'

'So you'd know whether he actually got killed in the explosion or was still alive.'

'We would,' she said.

'More port, anyone?' Martin asked, holding up the bottle.

During one of our shifts while they were sleeping I'd popped the back off the framed happy snap in the galley. It was a machine-made colour print and printed on the back besides the name of the photolab, 'Wing-On Photo, Macau', there was the usual colour correction information and a date. It didn't tell me exactly when the photo was taken but it did tell me it was printed six months ago, which proved little except that Jack Stark might not have been quite as dead as rumour had it. And someone who knew what they were doing had chosen exactly the right mix of weaponry to defend this boat at sea.

But I could see I wasn't going to get any more information on Stark out of these two. I raised my glass once more. 'To bank-robbing bank managers, damsels in distress and to Jack Stark, wherever he is, dead or alive.'

After dinner I was stacking the dishes in the galley when Faith came in carrying a gun.

I held up my hands. 'Look, I *said* I'd do the dishes.'

She smiled and handed me the pistol. It was a neat little Walther, the PPK. Very James Bond.

'Thanks, but I've already got a gun,' I said.

'That Makarov's a piece of junk.'

She did have a point. And the PPK or Polizeipistole Kriminalmodell is an excellent little gun for something with such a great big name.

'The price on your head has gone up to half a million,' she said. 'That's for the off-the-books players. ASIO, ASIS and D-E-D have you listed as a person of "Extreme Interest".'

I'd thought I was overvalued at two hundred and fifty thousand, but I was appreciating faster than a Double Bay penthouse with harbour views. 'Extreme Interest' was also a less than desirable category to find yourself in. The message implicit in 'Extreme Interest' was 'Wanted: Dead or Alive'. There were enough cowboys operating across the security services to make my future look decidedly ordinary. Shoot me full of holes and get a pat on the back and a promotion if you're an insider and the number of a fat Swiss bank account if you're a freelancer.

'How up-to-date is your information?' I asked.

She smiled. 'At three-seventeen this afternoon there was a reported sighting of someone answering your description on the *Spirit of Tasmania* forty-five minutes off docking at Station Pier in Melbourne. The SAS had three of their Tactical Assault Group hunter/killer teams onboard by three-thirty-nine.'

That must have made for quite a finale to the holidays of all those returning from the Apple Isle. And it was using a very big hammer to crack a very small nut. The TAG were usually reserved for major counter-terrorist operations and that didn't sound much like yours truly.

'Did they get me?' I asked.

'No,' she said, 'but they do want you bad.'

I nodded. 'You've got a satellite phone on board?'

'We do, but believe me, there isn't anyone you can call.'

'You're very well informed, for a retired librarian in the middle of the ocean.'

'Maybe I hear voices,' she said.

'From beyond the grave?' I asked.

'You catch on fast,' she said with a smile, 'for a photographer.'

TWENTY-SIX

Getting ashore in Broome was as easy as taking the zodiac in to the beach just after dawn and stepping back onto Australian soil. I'm sure if I'd been an Iranian national getting off a leaking Indonesian fishing boat there'd have been a bit of a fuss, but then again, since this wasn't an election year, maybe not.

Faith deftly ran the zodiac into the shallows and Martin held it steady while we leapt over the side and onto the beach, Grace doing her Navy Seal manoeuvre and me doing my Ashton's Circus seal version.

'Thanks again for everything, you two.'

'Glad to be of help,' Martin said. 'And remember, you've got an open invitation any time you're in Macau. Just look for the Pousada do Estoril.'

'Off Avenida Almeida Ribeiro, right?'

'You got it,' Faith said, turning the zodiac back into the

waves. 'You can't miss it. It's got a fantastic restaurant on the ground floor – place called "Jack's".'

She gunned the motor and they were gone.

We found transport down to Perth on the noticeboard of a backpacker hostel. For a share of the driving and fuel costs we crammed into the back seat of a twenty-five-year-old Ford station wagon that was carrying marginally less camping equipment than Captain Scott's ill-fated 1911 expedition to the South Pole. All we needed were some ponies.

The battered station wagon was older than the driver and was held together by bumper stickers and decals that indicated it had been everywhere, some places twice and three times. It was owned and operated by Hendrik, a scrawny young Dutchman from The Hague, and his spunky Swedish girlfriend Sigrid. Hendrik and Sigrid had met up several months earlier at the famous Bondi Christmas Day beach party and since then they had rooted themselves stupid in every backpacker hostel and campsite from Byron Bay to Bunbury. Now they were heading to Perth to sell the Ford and slowly bonk their way back to Europe, starting in Bali.

Holland is a very small country but from the way Hendrik drove no part of it would have been more than ninety seconds from his front door. Our presence in the back seat almost certainly restricted their usual on-the-road method of entertainment. The lovely Sigrid graciously kept her head above the level of the seat back at all times but as Grace pointed out at one rest stop, we couldn't really see what her hands were doing. When Hendrik was at the wheel he appeared to be a very happy little Dutchman. My suggestion that we play spotto to pass the time didn't get much of a response.

In Perth I gave them Mungo's address in Ubud, since he could use the business, and five hundred dollars US for the Ford. We waved goodbye at Perth Airport as they boarded a Denpasar-bound Garuda jet. The Ford obviously preferred the subtle touch of a clog on the accelerator since it seized up and died before we made it back into the centre of the city. I gave up on the car idea, found the Greyhound office on Wellington Street and bought two one-way tickets to Sydney.

The first white explorers crossed the Australian continent east to west by camel train. We were doing it west to east by bus and halfway into the second day I began wondering where I could get us a couple of camels. The whine of tyres on the asphalt, greasy truck-stop hamburgers and sleepless nights began to chip away at the feelings of well-being we'd developed while on the yacht.

My plan was to leave the bus at the last stop before the Sydney depot and then grab a suburban train into the city. I knew from experience that they'd be more likely to be watching interstate and international arrival and departure points than local railway stations. It was as good a plan as I could come up with, given the circumstances. If we crossed the city by train as far north as possible then we could flag down a bus headed for Byron Bay on the highway and get tickets onboard.

Like all good plans it didn't make any allowance for the intervention of a bunch of dickheads. I really think all the war colleges and military training centres where they do war gaming should have to have a large spanner labelled 'A Bunch of Dickheads' that they chuck into the works now and again. Our particular dickheads had mullets, moccasins and pegged jeans and were driving an old Sandman panel van. They rolled into the highway diner parking lot a few minutes after our driver had stopped for fuel and to allow us to grab a meal and stretch our legs.

It was past midnight and Grace and I were walking back across the deserted parking lot towards the empty bus when dickhead number one asked for a light. You can always see it coming and I looked longingly into the bus and up at the locker above our seats that held my spare pair of socks and the PPK. The driver and the rest of the passengers were still in the roadhouse finishing off their meals and if they had any sense they'd stay there. Dickhead number one didn't even wait for an answer about getting a light. The muzzle of his pistol looked to be about the same diameter as his extremely dilated pupils.

Dickheads two to four had joined us by this stage and they were also heavily armed and totally wasted. The odds were not good and the fact that they were high added an uncomfortable level of unpredictability to the situation. The newspapers seemed to be spot-on about the epidemic of guns and drugs. These bozos were carrying what used to be very expensive weapons which were way out of place in any old-fashioned parking-lot mugging. We put our hands up and I handed over my wallet.

Dickhead number one looked confused by the mix of Australian and US dollars for a moment, then he stuffed the notes into his pocket. He tossed the empty wallet onto the gravel at my feet. I was glad I'd tucked a couple of hundred bucks into my shoe.

Grace handed over her purse. I liked the fact that she had a purse. A purse and a laminated card giving you unfettered access to the American military machine were all that a girl really needed.

'It's a long ride to Sydney,' dickhead number one said, looking at Grace. 'You'll probably be more comfortable in the van with us.'

Grace shook her head. 'I'm happy on the bus.'

One of the other dickheads sniggered.

'It wasn't an invitation,' dickhead number one said.

'You boys are making a big mistake,' I said.

Dickhead number one pointed his pistol right between my eyes. 'And you should shut your fuckin' trap'.

'It's cool,' Grace said, touching my arm gently. 'I'll catch up with you later.'

One of the other dickheads sniggered again.

I shrugged. If dickhead number one hadn't been quite so

wasted he might have picked up on the tone in Grace's voice. As they walked towards the van she looked back at me and smiled. 'If you get lost, keep walking west.'

Where the hell did that come from?

Two of the dickheads got into the back of the Sandman with Grace while the third started the van and drove it over to us. The fourth backed over to the passenger-side door with his pistol still pointed vaguely in my direction.

'You know what's gunna happen if you call the cops,' he warned.

I shook my head. 'I won't be calling the cops,' I said, and I did have a fair idea of what was going to happen.

They were long gone by the time the driver and the rest of the passengers ambled back to the bus. No-one noticed we were one short when we pulled out of the parking lot.

The driver and I were probably the only two who were awake an hour later when the bus slowed down to carefully navigate its way around a single-car accident. There were lots of flashing lights on the tow trucks and ambulances and highway patrol cars. Police officers in reflective yellow vests were directing traffic. A crew from a local volunteer fire brigade were enthusiastically working on dousing the flames enveloping the battered Sandman, which had apparently run off the road into a ditch.

As we crawled past I could see ambulance paramedics doing frantic CPR on one of the dickheads. Two more were sitting on the verge with their backs to the road and handcuffs around their wrists. A police sergeant with his Glock drawn was keeping a very close eye on them. Dickhead number one was sitting on the tailgate of an ambulance. From the way his arms hung down limply at his sides I could tell they were both broken. He was crying and I guessed with good reason. It really must have hurt like a bastard.

There was no sign of Grace but I wasn't too fussed. Good-looking girl like her wouldn't have had any trouble hitching a ride. The poor dills in the Sandman had had no idea what they were getting themselves into. The moment they drove off with her I just knew it was going to end in tears.

TWENTY-SEVEN

We hit Sydney a little earlier than I expected and although daylight savings had just ended, it was still a touch too bright for my liking. To kill some time and keep a low profile I joined a bus tour that included a shiny silver metallic wig in the ticket price. 'Queens Of The Road' visits the entertainment hotspots and cultural icons of Sydney while drag-queen tour guides perform a tribute to *Priscilla, Queen of the Desert*. I bought the deluxe package, which just about cleaned me out but got me champagne and canapés along with my wig. The itinerary included Bondi Beach and I intended to sneak away from the group there. I was probably going to need all my years of espionage experience to pull this off since the tour was run by a group of very attractive men in drag who had it organised like a NASA space-shuttle launch.

It was still early when we swung through the Cross and Darlene, our tour leader, promised a return leg later on when things had hotted up. Kings Cross is Sydney's square mile of sin and it's not too bad early in the evening: neon and strip-joints and fast-food outlets and the odd bored-looking prostitute lounging outside some crummy hotel. The whole joint would be jumping later though and later still, probably around sunrise, you could cruise on through the saddest square mile you'd ever be likely to see.

Darlene, who was probably Daryl in daylight, looked fetching in an above-the-knee orange Dior A-line sixties knockoff. She was trying to get me to take the microphone and lead the bus in a rendition of ABBA's 'Take a Chance on Me' when we passed The Bourbon and I spotted Gordon and Sheldon at a window table deep in discussion. This was excellent timing since karaoke isn't really my thing. I handed Darlene my champagne glass.

'Sorry, gorgeous,' I said, 'but I've got to go. Something's come up.'

Darlene fluttered her false eyelashes and shook her head. 'Story of my life, duckie,' she said in a husky falsetto. 'Keep the wig, it suits you. Makes you look very extinguished.'

She yelled to the driver to pull over opposite the El Alamein Fountain and gave me a big smooch as a penalty before letting me off. After the bus pulled back into the traffic with all the passengers waving and the 'girls' blowing kisses, I glanced at my reflection in a souvenir-shop window. Dishevelled clothing from a cross-country bus trip, metallic silver wig and a big red lipstick kiss on my cheek. I looked around and bugger me if I didn't fit right in. I was practically invisible.

I grabbed a hot-dog from a vendor opposite The Bourbon and found a doorway where I could loiter and keep an eye on Sheldon and Gordon. The Bourbon was a restaurant and bar that had become famous in the sixties as The Bourbon & Beefsteak when Sydney was a hot destination for war-weary GIs on R and R from Vietnam. The place had a colourful history but now it had new owners who had ditched the Beefsteak and taken it decidedly upmarket. Not so upmarket that they wouldn't let Sheldon and Gordon sit in the window though. There was a girl at the table with them who looked about nineteen or twenty and very bored. While Sheldon and Gordon had their heads together she was chatting on a mobile phone and smoking. Talk about bad tradecraft. A window seat and a live mobile at the same table. If Byron had been here he could have stolen every single word of what was being said.

Lacking Byron's presence, I had to try to figure what was going on from the body language. Gordon wasn't happy. He made a call on his mobile and then handed a credit card to the waiter. By the time he'd signed the credit card slip and pocketed the receipt a Com Car was waiting at the kerb. So this was a business meeting, or at least that's what it would say on Gordon's expenses form and on the Com Car log. More bad tradecraft. Gordon was leaving a trail like a bulldozer crossing a bowling green.

Sheldon and the girl left right after Gordon. I decided to

follow them as they headed down a side street and into a parking station. The place was gloomy and the parking bays were only half full since the recent rash of armed robberies had turned into a full-blown epidemic. They stopped by a red Porsche Carrera and the indicators flashed as Sheldon hit the 'Unlock' button on his keys. The girl slid into the passenger seat, showing a lot of thigh. She looked very expensive. I wondered if Sheldon was putting *her* on his expenses. Mrs Asher and all the little Ashers had only lasted six months into Sheldon's Australian posting and had then moved back to the townhouse in Washington. The story was she wanted to be near her ailing mother.

Sheldon stood by the open driver's-side door and put both hands on the roof. For a moment I wondered if the girl was about to showcase some of her undoubted talents for him from inside the car but then he spoke.

'Nothing up my sleeves, buddy boy, and I'm pretty sure you've got something nasty aimed my way, so why don't we just chat.'

I stayed in the shadows behind a pillar. The Carrera's interior light was on and I could see the girl's head bopping to music coming through headphones. If Sheldon had spotted me then he was better than I expected or *my* tradecraft was slipping. My money was on the latter.

'Gordon's worried about you, buddy boy,' Sheldon continued. 'After what happened to Harry, we all are.' His southern accent made him sound almost sincere.

'Worried enough to put me in a red folder?' I asked.

Sheldon shook his head. 'You have to see it from his point of view. Until you come in and help us figure out what's going on then everyone's a suspect.'

'Including you?'

Sheldon smiled a tight smile. 'I am, of course, as a representative of the US government above reproach but I stand ready to assist Gordon in any way possible to resolve this situation.'

'That's great,' I said. 'I think I'd enjoy hooking you up to a high-voltage generator and asking a few questions.'

His smile was even tighter this time.

'You want to tell me what's really going on, Sheldon?'

He turned his palms upward. 'It's a mystery to me.'

'Hands back flat on the duco, please,' I said. 'At this range I can't miss.'

Sheldon did as I asked. 'You are out on a limb, buddy boy,' he said after a moment. 'It's a very long limb and people are starting to saw through it. Maybe you should just call Gordon and arrange to meet someplace.'

'Not in this lifetime,' I said. 'I'm going for a walk. You know the drill.'

Sheldon nodded. 'Keep my hands on the roof and count to one hundred.'

I racked the slide on the PPK, cocking it. 'Make it *three* hundred.'

'And you'll hang around for the first hundred to make sure I'm playing the game?'

'Something like that. You'll just have to decide if you want to find out.'

'You wanna do me a favour, buddy boy?' Sheldon asked.

I didn't answer.

'Leave the wig. I think my young friend here might look kinda cute in it.'

Jesus. Maybe Sheldon *was* better than I thought.

TWENTY-EIGHT

Blowing five hundred bucks on Hendrik's near-death station wagon was an expense I hadn't counted on. Then the transcontinental bus trip, the robbery on the highway and the 'Queens Of The Road' ticket had almost totally cleaned me out. The only thing left in my cover identity's wallet was fifty bucks and a debit card linked to a bank with an ATM handy to my apartment in Bondi. I wanted to sneak a peek at the place anyway to see if they had any surveillance on it and I figured I could use the opportunity to cash up for the trip to Byron.

It was after two in the morning when I wound up on a nearly deserted Campbell Parade. After I paid the taxi I was down to thirty bucks. A careful check of the area showed no sign of any watchers. No overt surveillance didn't mean I would be crazy enough to go into my flat but I was willing to risk pulling some cash out of the ATM. The card was in my cover identity's name but just in case someone was monitoring the camera in the ATM I decided on one more diversion. I guess my paranoia was reaching record levels but after the last few days I felt it was justified.

A street kid was sleeping in a bus shelter at the end of the main drag. Waking him wasn't easy. He was about seventeen with a junkie's pallor and that look that says he probably doesn't have too long to live. He was a little wary of the deal at first – $50 of the $1000 I wanted from the machine. His bleary eyes sized me up and I knew he was working out if he could outrun me with the whole bundle so I opened my jacket and showed him the butt of the pistol in my belt. The kid took the ATM card and repeated my four-digit PIN half a dozen times out loud before shuffling towards the machine. He glanced back a couple of times, probably to make sure he wasn't hallucinating.

I waited in the doorway of an Indian take-away, out of the wind and out of line of sight of the autoteller, while he botched his first two attempts to key in the PIN. There was no traffic and the Parade was silent apart from the sound of waves breaking down on the beach. The kid was certainly making a meal of a simple job. He shuffled back to my doorway to confirm whether the last two digits were five nine or nine five. I picked up a discarded menu from the Indian restaurant and wrote the number in big letters. If he screwed up this time and the machine ate my card I was rooted. I wondered if I should just make the withdrawal myself.

Back at the ATM the kid put the menu on the ledge and carefully studied the four numbers. He poked his tongue out of the corner of his mouth and deliberately and firmly pushed the buttons. I was starting to feel sorry for the poor little bugger and wondering what sort of future he had when the question almost became academic. The kid turned in my direction and gave the thumbs-up, smiling happily. He'd finally keyed in the number correctly. Then he stared at the screen for a moment and turned and began walking back towards me. Jesus, what now?

He started to yell. 'Was it cheque or sav . . . ?'

The shock wave from the explosion cut off the question and shattered almost every shop window on the block. Being tucked well back into a doorway saved me from any flying glass but I was slammed against the brick wall of the alcove. When I staggered out onto the footpath my ears were ringing. There was a smoking hole in the wall where the ATM had been and the wailing of shop and car burglar alarms filled the moment of dead silence that immediately followed the blast. Directly opposite the ATM, a car parked at the kerb was over on its side out on the roadway and I could smell petrol. It was obviously a directional charge, with a short delay while the detonator circuit confirmed the cardholder's ID number before triggering.

The kid was flat on his face, but at least he was breathing. I checked his pulse and looked for any broken bones and bleeding but there were only some superficial cuts, despite all the flying glass, so I figured he might be just mildly concussed. Lucky little bugger. He opened his eyes and gave me a glassy stare.

'Do I have to go to school today, Mum?' he said.

I took that as a good sign and dragged him across the pavement, propping him up against a parking meter. After checking his pulse again I gave him a couple of light slaps on the face.

He groaned and then mumbled, 'Wa'happen?'

'Luckiest day of your life, sport. You should buy yourself a lottery ticket.' I pushed twenty bucks into his jacket pocket. It was the best I could do. No point in yelling for someone to dial 000 – the emergency service's number was probably in meltdown right about now. Besides, the Bondi cop shop was just around the corner so he wouldn't have long to wait for help.

I found a vacant cab at a rank four blocks from the beach. The cabbie was reading a book on fly fishing and he had the radio up full tilt, which was probably why he hadn't heard the explosion. He gave me a strange look when I got in and when I checked in the rear-view mirror there was blood on my face. Mine or the kid's? I looked to see if I was bleeding anywhere else and that's when I found the Walther was missing. Bugger.

We headed towards the Cross. I figured I'd just see how

close ten bucks and change would get me and then walk the rest of the way. It was a noisy and colourful ride. It seemed like every fire engine and emergency-services vehicle in the eastern suburbs was screaming back towards the beach with lights and sirens going full tilt.

When I got out of the taxi near the empty Kings Cross fire station I was unarmed and flat broke. My gun was somewhere back on Campbell Parade along with about ten thousand dollars from the ATM. I could really have used some of that cash right now but it would take a long time and a really big roll of sticky tape to put it all back together.

Had the bastards wired every damn autoteller in the country just to get me? What was worse was I'd used a supposedly clean ATM card that theoretically wasn't linked to me. And they obviously didn't care if I was lining up with twenty mums and dads on a Saturday morning. Christ, even Mrs T used that machine a couple of times a week. I was really glad I'd warned her off going into my flat. Who knows what was waiting on the other side of my front door.

Lothar wasn't too pleased to see what was waiting on the other side of *his* front door but he must have figured that opening it was the only way to stop the banging.

'It's bloody three o'clock in the morning, you know, Mr Murdoch,' he said. 'What are my neighbours going to think?'

That was rich. Lothar's Motel Double-D Luxe was four

floors of squalor down a dismal and dimly lit side street where even the Rottweilers kept pit bulls for protection. Rooms in this run-down sixties fire-trap rented by the hour and in every one of those hours there was banging on doors by drunks, the drug squad, pimps or ripped-off punters, and ambulance officers called to shoot Narcan into a collapsed vein to revive yet another OD'd junkie. Harry used to say Lothar should just keep Narcan in the minibars to save everyone a lot of trouble. *Not* having someone hammer on your door after midnight made you look suspicious in this roach motel.

Lothar unlocked the steel security door and let me in. The living room was crammed with bulging garbage bags, piles of old newspapers and mounds of wrinkled clothing. Pornographic magazines and videotapes were stacked up haphazardly on top of the ancient TV and the sink in the small kitchen was hidden under empty pizza boxes and half empty plastic take-away containers from the local Chinese. I'd seen third world rubbish dumps with more appeal than this place.

Skinny, bordering on anorexic, Lothar had wispy yellow hair that appeared to be falling out in clumps, bad skin and even worse teeth. Though probably a few years younger than me he seemed to be hovering somewhere between ninety and death. Over his grubby flannel pyjamas he was wearing a disgusting threadbare, torn and badly stained dressing gown. I made a mental note that if I ever found myself wearing a dressing gown like that I'd end it all, right then and there.

'I need a gun.'

Lothar pulled the dressing gown around his scrawny body and studied my scratched face. 'I'll bet you do,' he said.

Lothar was usually scared of me, which is why he called me Mr Murdoch, like I was a cop. There was an edge of bravado in his voice now which told me he knew I was fair game out on the streets. We stared at each other and he looked away first.

'I'm not in that game any more,' he said, and the bravado was gone. 'Honestly.'

'Honestly?' I said. 'Jesus, Lothar, give me a break.'

Lothar, besides being in the hospitality industry, was well known as the man you went to for a discreet purchase or short-time rental of your reliable and concealable handguns.

'It's true, Mr Murdoch,' he went on, 'the game's stuffed. I used to sell quality merchandise at a fair price and now all of a sudden the streets are flooded with cheap automatics and cheap dope and it ain't worth it no more. They're all crazy out there. People won't pay what the stuff is really worth and if you give them an argument they're just as likely to shoot you as tell you to fuck off.'

I almost felt sorry for him. But if he thought it was bad out on his side of the street he should try walking on mine. 'Things are tough all over, Lothar, but I need a gun. Now.'

He looked like he was going to give me an argument but changed his mind and took down an old bakelite canister marked *Biscuits* from the top shelf of a sideboard. Under some stale milk arrowroots was a package wrapped in a dirty tea towel. He unwrapped the tea towel and handed me a battered little Beretta .25 semi-automatic. It almost made me wistful for the Makarov.

'Ned Kelly not need this any more?'

'Berettas is good guns,' he said, 'even the old ones. You know that, Mr Murdoch.'

He was right on that score. But this little piece was from way back in the pre–safety catch days. I checked the action. 'Ammo's not the same vintage, I hope?'

He handed me a shiny new box of cartridges. 'Two-fifty's fair, with the bullets.'

I nodded. 'You'd probably get five hundred from a museum.' I loaded the clip and slipped the gun and spare ammunition into my jacket pocket. 'However, I'm a bit strapped for cash, Lothar, so I'm going to have to owe you. In fact, I need you to lend me a fifty.'

Lothar studied me for a moment. 'I want your watch.' Some of the bravado was back.

I glanced at the vintage stainless steel Omega Seamaster on my wrist. 'You're asking me for collateral, Lothar, after all we've been through together?'

'It's fair, given the circumstances. Let's face it, Mr Murdoch, you're not exactly a long-term proposition at the moment.'

I unsnapped the metal band and handed him the watch. 'I'll be coming back, so don't sell it, you little prick, or you're history.' I probably sounded a lot more positive than I felt.

He put the watch in a desk drawer and gave me a fifty.

I stopped in the dank hallway and looked back at him. 'You know what will happen if you tell anyone I was here, Lothar?'

He nodded. 'I'll be a very, very rich man,' he said, and he slammed the heavy steel door shut. He grinned at me through the bars. 'And you'll be dead, Mr Murdoch . . . d-e-d dead.'

The morning sun was just lighting the tips of the Norfolk pines along Manly beach when I reached out of the bus shelter on the promenade and grabbed the girl's arm. I was ready for the reaction but she was even quicker and more agile than I'd anticipated and I hit the ground hard. Luckily for me she went for the face rather than the groin so the damage was minimal by the time she recognised me and pulled her punch.

'You're a fucking dickhead, Alby,' she said through gritted teeth. The heel of the palm of her right hand was only centimetres from my face. 'Another half-second and you'd have had your nose bone in your brain.'

I appreciated the helping hand as she pulled me up from the footpath. Julie looked great in her tight shorts and singlet, even if she had just run ten kilometres. I'd been watching the whole time, just to make sure no-one else was watching too.

'I've always admired your restraint when it comes to me,' I said.

'Don't flatter yourself,' she snapped. 'If I'd followed through with the punch, right about now I'd be eligible for a three-grade seniority bump, a cash bonus and a week on Hayman Island, all expenses paid.'

That was disappointing. Only a week. 'Parasailing included in that?' I asked.

Julie's sister Michelle was night manager at a schmick hotel on the Corso and she gave us an ocean-view room without any of the usual formalities. She also sent up an excellent room-service breakfast for two. I ate both breakfasts while Julie took a shower. She came out of the bathroom in a terry towelling robe and scowled at the wreckage on the room-service trolley.

'I saved you an orange juice,' I said.

She shook her head. 'You're in such deep shit it's unbelievable.'

'We can get Mish to send up another breakfast,' I suggested.

'Alby,' she said slowly, 'you need to wake up to yourself. Some very nasty people want you dead. And they don't care who they hurt in the process. So right now you are not only in a lot of danger but you're also very much a danger to anybody within a ten-metre radius of your sorry arse.'

'You're right.' She *was* right. And she was fifteen years younger than me, which made it worse. Nothing makes you feel older than a younger person telling you to behave. 'Any idea what Harry was into?'

She shook her head. 'He asked me to check a few things on the Springs, nothing heavy. Harry was a straight arrow, you know that. If it was anything I wasn't cleared for he wouldn't have talked about it. Not even in bed.'

'Were you two serious?' I asked.

She smiled a sad smile. 'Not really. But he was a funny guy. And nice. I was really surprised. You dedheads always come across as such a bunch of macho arseholes.'

I was really feeling guilty about that second breakfast now. I offered her a piece of leftover toast. She took it.

'Have you got a handle on what's going on?'

'It's all on a "need to know" basis,' she said, 'and it looks like the only people who really need to know anything are Sheldon and Gordon.'

'How's Rutherford doing? Still in a coma?'

She nodded. 'When we heard about your camera cases blowing up on the tarmac Graeme threw a serious wobbly in Gordon's office. The bit I overheard was about your gear being picked up by someone named Buzz, who wasn't one of our regular couriers, and Graeme wanting to know who had authorised it. After he left Gordon got straight on the phone to Sheldon.'

'Shit!' Not much got past Graeme and by confronting Gordon he'd made himself a target. This was getting very ugly and our fearless leader was obviously up to his neck in whatever the hell was going on.

'There's more,' Julie continued. 'The two hoodlums who got shot along with Harry in Double Bay had various business interests in the Cross . . . including The Ice Chest.'

For a moment I thought I was going to throw up. 'Holy hell!'

'My thoughts exactly,' Julie said.

I walked across to the window and looked out at the beach and the promenade and the famous Norfolk pines. The old, pre-metric tourism slogan for Manly used to be *'Seven miles from the city and a thousand miles from care'*. Not today it bloody wasn't.

'Anything on Grace Goodluck?'

'I checked with a contact at the Agency in Sydney when I got back', she said, 'off the record. Dark hair, olive skin, tall, good cheekbones and fantastic tits?' she asked.

'I couldn't possibly comment on her breasts,' I said.

Julie looked shocked. 'I'll be damned. Don't tell me all that gender equity training has finally kicked in?'

'What can I say? I'm a sensitive new-age spy.'

Julie smiled. 'Anyway,' she went on, 'it seems like a woman answering that description had a face-to-face with Sheldon last week.' She paused. 'Or maybe that should be a *chest*-to-face.'

I made a *tsk tsk* sound and she smiled again.

'He was apparently having kittens after she left and pulled a file with the codename Mankiller.'

I poured myself another coffee. The more I found out

about this the less things made sense. Was Grace CIA, and if she was, what was she meeting with Sheldon about? And if she was Mankiller then why were her own people out looking for her? And did the name Mankiller carry any extra significance that should make me more worried than I already was?

'I need some cash,' I said.

Julie nodded. 'I heard about the malfunction at the ATM. I'll get some money off Mish and fix her up later. What are you going to do?'

I shook my head. 'It's better that you don't know.'

'Okay,' she said. 'Just promise me you'll keep your head down. Sheldon and Gordon are both screaming national security so the state and federal cops have to do what they tell them.' She poured herself what was left of the coffee.

'Who was it that said patriotism is the last refuge of scoundrels?' I said.

Julie took a sip of her coffee. 'I'm pretty sure it was Gordon's mum.'

TWENTY-NINE

By the time the overnight bus got into Byron Bay it was a toss-up as to what smelled worse – me or the onboard toilet. My ten-dollar plastic truck-stop sunglasses helped filter out some of the morning light as I found the ocean, stripped down to my jocks and fell in. Putting my trousers back on, I let the breeze dry me as I walked along Wattego's Beach, searching for Charlie Somersby's house. I chose the oldest in sight as I knew he was a long-time resident.

Charlie had trained in Canada under the Empire Air Training Scheme in the forties and was a pilot on combat operations with the RAF before his twenty-first birthday. He'd flown black-painted Halifax bombers over Nazi-occupied Europe very low and very late at night, doing all sorts of skulduggery for a special-duties squadron in the Second Tactical Air Force. After surviving the war he'd come home to Australia and taken up commercial flying.

In the late fifties Charlie was piloting the big Sandringham flying boats out of Rose Bay in Sydney, flying holiday-makers to island resorts on the Barrier Reef. One day, between flights, he got a telegram saying that a titled lady back in England with an estate not too many miles from Charlie's old airfield had died and left him half a million quid. No-one could ever figure out exactly what Charlie's connection to the aristocracy had entailed but he packed up his flying gear and never set foot on an aircraft again.

He'd moved to Byron in the sixties and began dabbling with early computers as a hobby and very quickly had become an expert. Through his wartime contacts he'd been brought into the Defence Department in the seventies to consult on computerisation but hadn't done anything official for the last decade as far as I knew.

A battered V-Dub kombi van covered in colourfully painted palm trees was parked at the gate. There was an airbrushed illustration of three pretty hula dancers on the van's side and the carefully lettered sign 'Lovely Hula Hands – Massage & Holistic Healing'. The front gate of the house was open and as I walked up the stairs to the verandah I could hear music. A knock on the screen door brought a gruff voice inviting me in.

The early-morning light was coming through wooden venetian slats, illuminating Charlie and the three people I took to be from Lovely Hula Hands. Charlie was tanned and fit for an eighty-something-year-old; he probably swam every day from the look of him and given his proximity to the beach.

There was incense burning and the scent of fresh flowers. One of the Hula ladies was sitting on a cane chair strumming a ukulele, while the other two were on the floor in the middle of the room, massaging oil into Charlie's prostrate body. It was an idyllic scene. Everyone was wearing flower leis around their necks. No-one was wearing anything else. I began to wonder if my pension would ever stretch to a beach house in the area.

Charlie looked up, trying to place me. 'You're that friend of Harry's, aren't you?' he said. 'Alby, right? Pour yourself a drink. You look like something the cat dragged in.'

News travels slowly in the north. He hadn't heard about the shooting in Double Bay. When I told him he wrapped himself in a sarong and bundled the girls out to the van. After he waved them off he made me a huge breakfast, which we ate in silence on the verandah. There was Scotch in the coffee and it mellowed me out quickly.

'Do you always start the day with three naked women?'

He laughed. 'Good heavens, no. I'm on a fixed income!'

I knew from Harry that Charlie had made some shrewd investments with his half-million quid but he took great delight in screwing every possible cent he could from the Department of Veterans' Affairs.

'I do have a regular booking every Thursday, though. That's pension day – they give me 10 per cent off.'

That made about as much sense as everything else that had happened lately.

We took the whisky bottle for a walk along the beach and he told me about Harry's last visit. In checking the CIA-supplied personnel records from the Springs Harry had come across something that didn't make sense and he'd been concerned enough to drive to Byron to talk it over with Charlie.

'So what caught his attention?'

Charlie picked up a flat stone and skimmed it out across the ocean. 'Birthday cakes, and lots of them.'

I looked at him. Harry had talked about birthdays on his answerphone tape. 'Okay,' I said, 'I'll bite. Birthday cakes?'

Charlie nodded and sat down on the sand. I joined him.

'As you probably know,' he explained, 'the Americans fly all their food into the Springs. Nearest supermarket's in Darwin and I'm sure it doesn't stock cheese in a spray can and Oreos and peanut butter cups and all the other dreadful things those people eat.' He shuddered. 'So the Globemasters wobble in twice a month to deliver the mail and top up the larder. Three hundred people can get through a lot of frozen pizza.'

I waited. Charlie was getting there, even if he seemed to be taking the long way round.

'Harry was about to wrap up his vetting of the personnel files when he picked up something odd in his copy of the print-out.'

'How odd?'

'December fourth, last year, Harry calculated they would have needed an extra flight into the Springs just for all the birthday cakes.'

I looked at him. It wasn't making any more sense than his 10 per cent pensioner discount story.

Charlie leaned over to me. 'According to the computer print-out the Americans gave Harry, forty-one out of the three hundred staff at the base were going to have their birthdays on December fourth.'

I considered the implications. Charlie looked at me and nodded. 'No-one in his right mind would ever even consider putting that many Sagittarians in a small enclosed space, would they? Recipe for disaster.'

I nodded in agreement.

'What do you know about computers?' Charlie asked.

'I can turn one on.'

Charlie smiled. 'Very amusing. Do linear congruential random number generators and the Kolmogorov–Smirnov test mean anything to you?'

'I failed the Smirnov test in a couple of pubs in my younger days.'

Charlie shook his head sadly. 'Okay, let's talk computers and random numbers, but I'll try to keep it simple.'

Thank God for that. The second whisky was starting to kick in and on top of an overnight bus trip it wasn't a good feeling.

'Computers are great at logic,' Charlie explained, 'but they fall down a bit when it comes to randomness. This isn't a problem if you're say an accountant or a passenger on an airliner with a computer-controlled flight deck. In that case non-randomness is a very good thing. With me so far?'

I nodded. 'Sort of.'

'The truth is, computers are actually lousy at picking random numbers and, in fact, people are just as bad. We tend to either unconsciously insert patterns, or try too hard to avoid patterns, which is itself a pattern. But for most purposes computer-generated figures that are "statistically random" rather than "truly random" are good enough.'

'Now you're starting to lose me,' I said. Five more minutes of this and my ears would start bleeding.

'Okay, in Harry's case what it seemed to boil down to was a computer choosing names and dates at random.' He looked at me. 'Perhaps inventing three hundred people to serve at a hardship posting?'

That made me sit up. 'You mean like the Springs?'

Charlie nodded. 'But as I said, a computer can be bad at random. Would it know enough to spot a non-random sequence? If it was programmed to look for it, it might. But in this case something messed up. And badly. Somehow, against all odds, the computer that generated that personnel list for the Springs randomly spat out exactly the same birth date forty-one times, which in a group of three hundred is statistically highly improbable.'

'Bugger me.'

'Harry picked it up,' Charlie went on, 'simply because whoever organised the list in the first place hadn't. Operator error. What it comes down to is that the personnel list for the base at Bitter Springs is as screwy as a two-bob watch.'

He shook his head sadly. 'First thing I ever told Harry about computers – they're 100 per cent reliable, except when they're not.'

Harry had spent the night in Byron before driving back to Sydney. He planned to fly down to Melbourne to talk to Gordon about why the Americans would give us a phoney staff list. Charlie had the good sense to ask that his name be kept out of the discussions, which was probably why he was still alive and kicking. Obviously D-E-D was leaking like a sieve. My taking the next bus out might help to keep old Charlie healthy for a little longer. At the very least until his next encounter with that multi-talented trio from Lovely Hula Hands.

THIRTY

Three days of hitchhiking and now I was standing in the middle of the desert waiting to die. It wasn't the way my cunning plan was supposed to work out, but so far it was par for the course. After the meeting with Charlie it was clear that the Springs had to be the next stop. Since I was now leery of any form of regular transport I'd been using my thumb and with quite reasonable success.

The cattle truck had dropped me around eight in the morning at the intersection of two roads that seemed to come from nowhere and lead to nowhere. The music in the cab of the big Kenworth was Gilbert and Sullivan, which wasn't what I'd expected but was a change from the country music that had assaulted my delicate sensibilities on all the other rides. The truck driver had left me with a two-litre bottle of water, which was all he could spare. I probably should have stayed with him but he was heading several hundred k's out of my way.

The intersection featured half-a-dozen home-made letterboxes for the cattle properties in the area. They'd all been shot full of holes by passing travellers with nothing better to do. I was tempted to pull out the little Beretta and fire a few myself. Must have been the isolation.

I finished off the last of the water five hours later when I saw the car. My lucky day, I decided. Out here no-one would refuse you a ride and anyone with any sense had plenty of water to spare. It was a big Ford, the one with all the creature comforts, and as it rolled to a stop the passenger window slid smoothly down, releasing a wave of chilled air.

'Need a ride, buddy boy?' the driver asked.

Maybe it wasn't my lucky day after all, but what choice did I have?

'Thanks, Sheldon,' I said as I slid into the comfort of the air-conditioning and the leather seats. 'You're a lifesaver.'

Sheldon pushed the car up to a hundred and twenty before I even had my seatbelt fastened. I tried to figure what were the odds that he had just happened by, but I gave up when I realised I couldn't think of a number big enough.

'Lifesaver, eh,' he said with one of those insincere laughs of his, 'that mean I've got a hole in my middle, buddy boy?'

We can but live in hope, I said to myself. I was glad I hadn't wasted any of the Beretta's bullets on those letterboxes.

'There's plenty of beer and Coke in there,' he said, indicating an electrically powered chiller sitting on the back seat. 'Water too, if that's your thing.'

I helped myself to some water. I actually could have murdered a beer but when a man like Sheldon Asher unexpectedly picks you up in the middle of the Australian desert you really want to keep your wits about you. I'd tried to ration the water the truckie had left me while I was waiting by the road but I was fairly sure I'd been sweating more out than had been going in. One of Sheldon's chilled half-litre bottles went down without even touching the sides.

'You've been causing a whole mess of trouble for my buddy Gordon, Mr Murdoch. It's a shame you didn't take my advice to come in.'

'Nothing personal, Sheldon, but until I know what happened to Harry and my camera cases I'm not taking anyone's advice.' I opened another bottle of water. 'The CIA have any theories about what went down?' I asked.

'That's a job for your local security services,' he said. 'The Agency wouldn't dream of interfering in the internal workings of a friendly sovereign nation.' He didn't even smile. The spy school at Langley probably has a class where you chant it like a mantra, over and over, till you can say it with a straight face. I'm sure the diehards even get to believe it eventually.

'With friends like you, Sheldon . . . ' I said. I didn't bother to finish the thought.

'Now, don't be like that, buddy boy. Where would you be if I hadn't come along right now? Not a whole lot of passing traffic out here.'

He was right about the traffic but I was starting to feel

that I'd have been better off taking my chances back at the crossroads.

'We headed to the Springs?' I asked. We appeared to be driving west but with the sun directly overhead it was hard to tell.

Sheldon shook his head slowly. 'I just don't know for the life of me why so many people are interested in that place all of a sudden.'

'You mean people like Grace Goodluck?'

'Quite a piece of work, that one,' Sheldon said.

'She one of yours?'

'Seems like,' Sheldon chuckled, 'but hey, in our business you can never be sure, eh, buddy boy?'

We didn't speak for the next half-hour. Sheldon just followed the road with the car in cruise control.

We eventually turned off onto a side track and then we left the track and drove across the sand. Sheldon seemed to know where he was going even if it looked to me that we had gone around in circles and were exactly in the middle of nowhere. The Ford had a GPS system built into the dashboard instrumentation so navigation shouldn't have been a problem. We finally stopped by a small rocky outcrop and Sheldon switched off the engine.

'Can you open the glove compartment?' he asked.

I did. There were no gloves, just a couple of maps and a small umbrella, but when I looked back at Sheldon he was pointing a compact Glock semi-automatic in my direction.

I got out of the car at his suggestion. I kept my hands away from my body, also at his suggestion. Sheldon was almost certainly an excellent shot. The CIA liked to keep its people's skills current in such areas. Reaching for the Beretta in my pocket would have been way too Hollywood. If he'd been unarmed I could have taken him. Sheldon was fit-looking and trim for his age but it was all exercise machine and protein-shake muscle. I'd once seen him take the elevator at his gym up three floors to a Stairmaster work-out.

'What the hell is going on, Sheldon?'

'When you and Harry stuck your noses into matters that didn't concern you, you made a lot of people unhappy and that's not good for business,' he said as he walked around and closed the passenger-side door. 'So you see, buddy boy, none of this is personal, it's just business.'

'Not politics?' I asked.

'Shoot, Alby,' he said, 'don't tell me you're still an idealist after all these years. Everything's business, I thought a bright boy like you would have figured that out by now.'

Shoot? Sheldon could kill someone in cold blood but he couldn't bring himself to use a curse word.

'Politicians come and go, my friend, but it's business and civil servants who endure,' he said. 'Once I figured that out I knew where I fit in the scheme of things.'

'Where exactly do you fit, Sheldon?'

He shrugged. 'You know way too much already, Alby. It's what's made you a liability, I'm afraid.'

What *did* I know? So far, only that there were too many people at Bitter Springs who were born on December 4. But the fact that Sheldon was here doing his own dirty work was a bit of a clue that whatever it was, he was in it up to his bolo tie.

'You wanna turn around and start walking, buddy boy?'

'Squeamish?' I asked. 'Harry got it front-on.'

'If it makes you feel any better,' he said, 'the guy who pulled the trigger on that one got wasted in a hotel driveway in Bali.'

He pronounced it 'Belly' but it was good news anyway. Julie would be pleased if she ever got to hear about it.

'Buzz Geiger, right?'

Sheldon nodded. 'We couldn't believe it when you and the girl turned up right on his doorstep. Nice little coincidence, that one.'

'Just like that nice little coincidence in Double Bay?'

'What coincidence is that, buddy boy?'

'Weren't the two hoods sitting in front of Harry at the Vienna your partners in The Ice Chest?'

'Ah, you see that's not so much of a coincidence. I prefer to look at it as more of a win/win situation. Three birds with one stone, isn't that the expression?'

So the rumour was true. And whatever reason Sheldon had for wanting to get rid of Harry he'd somehow managed to use it as a means of increasing his shareholding in a bloody nightclub. I wanted him dead so bad I could taste it.

Sheldon gestured with his pistol. 'Now I think it's time we took that little walk, buddy boy.'

I turned around and started walking. What else could I do? I walked fast, hoping to put as much distance between us as possible before the shooting started. Pistol accuracy drops off quite dramatically with distance and it was the only plan I could come up with. Just when I was about to drop into a crouch and start running the first bullet ripped past my ear, followed immediately by the bang from Sheldon's Glock. My roll to the left was automatic and when I came up with the Beretta blazing I think Sheldon and I were equally surprised.

His second and third bullets went wide and all six of mine splintered the glass of the passenger window. If the windows were bulletproof then the doors would be more so but my fusillade kept Sheldon's head down till I made it to the shelter of the rocks. Now we were even: he had his bulletproof car to hide behind and I had my bulletproof rock. The major advantage of Sheldon's hiding place became apparent though when I heard the car door slam and the engine start. The vehicle took off in a cloud of dust.

Blazing away with my pistol at the rapidly departing Ford was an option but definitely a waste of ammunition.

There was no point in walking so I sat down and waited. It was at least one hundred and fifty clicks to the Springs and there was nothing between here and there except desert. It was early afternoon and still about forty degrees centigrade. Sheldon hadn't managed to shoot me but driving off was going to achieve exactly the same result. If I didn't freeze during the night I was almost certain to dehydrate by noon tomorrow. Pity I hadn't guzzled a lot more water from Sheldon's cooler while I had the chance.

THIRTY-ONE

When I was certain Sheldon wasn't coming back I took stock of the situation, which didn't take too long. No food, no water, and no idea of where the hell I was – except that it was somewhere in the middle of the desert. The first rule of survival is that you stay right where you are so that the search parties can come to you but, since no-one was looking, that one was out the window. I could just sit still to conserve energy and fluids but where would that get me? And walking was just as much a death sentence as sitting and doing nothing; it would only speed things up a bit.

When I moved around the rock to get into some shade I found the dingo. Dead as a doornail and completely desiccated. So now I knew exactly how dry a dead dingo's donger was – pretty damn dry. That would be me before too long. There was a taller outcrop of rocks about a kilometre away that would offer more shade and as I walked to it I tried to remember the signs of dehydration. Extreme thirst was the first, and I already had that. Then would come dry, warm skin, dizziness, cramping in the arms and legs, headaches and a dry mouth and dry tongue with thick saliva. All these symptoms would get worse over time and eventually lead to hypovolaemic shock where the body's life-support systems start to slowly shut down. Hypovolaemic shock and what came after was pretty grim. Sometimes it's not a great idea to pay close attention to the survival briefings.

By the time I reached the shade of the big rock I was really thirsty and beginning to get light-headed. There was more dead wildlife, a small wallaby this time. When I sat down in the shade a large crow swooped out of the sky and landed on the rock above my head. Its glossy black feathers reminded me of Grace's hair sweeping down across her bare shoulder that night in Ubud. Where was she now? She'd sorted out the dills in the Sandman, which I knew she would, but what would her next move be? I remembered the way she smiled as they took her to the van. Then she'd said something. My fuzzy brain searched around for a moment and it came back in startling clarity. I shivered. 'If you get lost, keep walking west.' The crow cawed once and took off, black wings beating, and then it was gone. What did I have to lose? I asked myself, getting slowly to my feet. The sun was lower in the sky now, so the long shadows told me which way was west.

The ute came up quickly, billowing a huge cloud of bulldust that rolled forward to envelope me when the vehicle slewed to a stop. It was a battered old blue Valiant Wayfarer, as big as a battleship, with four Aboriginal men crammed in the front. The driver leaned out the window and smiled.

'Wanna ride?' he asked. It was a rhetorical question.

He jerked his thumb to the back and I climbed in with two more blokes, one sleeping, three dingo kelpie crosses also sleeping, and a dead kangaroo. The bloke in the back who was awake made room for me. He was about thirty, wearing jeans and old elastic-sided boots and a plaid shirt with the sleeves ripped off. Slimmer and slightly lighter-skinned than the four up front, he looked vaguely familiar. I must have been getting too much sun. He handed me a two-litre plastic bottle. The label said it was Vittel, premium mineral water from France, but the smell said it was out of an artesian bore. Apart from the smell and the taste and the fact that it was hot, it was delicious.

There was no back window in the ute cab and the radio was blaring. A commercial came on and the four blokes up front cheered and started singing along. And why not? That particular jingle had the whole country singing along the day after it came out. A sixties rock and roll song reworked to pitch peanut butter. With a hook that locked into your brain and wouldn't let go.

In the TV commercial a bunch of kids were eating peanut butter sandwiches and singing along to the tune of the Beach Boys' 'Good Vibrations':

Good, good, good pea-nut munchin'
Good, good, good pea-nut crunchin'
Nah, nah, nah, nah, nah, nah-nah nah . . .

But when they got to the nah-nah nah chorus, they could only hum along because the peanut butter had stuck their tongues to the roofs of their mouths. It was bloody brilliant. The four guys singing were having a ball so I turned to the bloke beside me and smiled.

'Great ad, that one, eh?' I said.

He looked up from the rifle he was cleaning and nodded. 'Perfect product launch,' he said. 'Zero to 22 per cent market share in three weeks. Fabulous demographics. By week five, it fell back to 4 per cent. The problem was the product tasted like shit.' He shook his head sadly. 'A bit of money spent on product research could have told them that.'

I think I must have had the same dopey expression on my face as the dead kangaroo.

'The boys like the ad a lot because I wrote it.' He gave me a wry smile, his teeth very white against his dark skin. 'My name's Terry.'

Of course it was. Now I could place the face.

'I'm Alby.'

'I know. Alby Murdoch. The goat picture, right?'

His full name was Terence Patrick Riley. Good Irish Catholic name for the first Aboriginal to be made a Creative Group Head in a major Australian ad agency. I'd read a lot about him in the trade papers. Kings School on a scholarship, and then a meteoric rise through the world of advertising. WORLDPIX had made a lot of money out of his campaigns. So had his clients. He'd won a swag of awards and the TV commercial for the crappy peanut butter got a Gold Lion at the Cannes advertising festival. He had it made. Two weeks before his transfer to head up the agency's New York office, he'd sold his penthouse flat, dropped the keys to his company BMW on the boardroom table and walked away.

The story was that he was living on a settlement in central Australia, working at preserving some of the traditional ways of his people. It looked like the story was true. We had a few friends in common in the industry and it turned out that Terry knew Byron from Kings so we chatted a little about work and friends but mostly we watched the scenery as the sun set. You only had to look around to know why he did it. Out here was the biggest sky in the world and mile after mile of the most spectacular nothingness you could imagine. There was a hypnotic magic to the emptiness. Dreamtime or primetime – I guess for Terry it was no contest.

An hour after sunset we hit a bitumen road. None too soon. The Valiant had bald tyres and on the soft dust of the bush tracks it had the handling characteristics of a slice of lime papaya pie. It handled somewhat better on the tar surface, perhaps a little more like a CWA lamington. There was a full moon and the driver didn't bother with headlights.

'It's the road to the satellite station at the Springs,' Terry yelled over the whine of the tyres on the bitumen. 'Connects with the airfield. The Yanks put it in years back.'

The track to their camp was about halfway between the base and the airfield. We turned off and drove another ten k's in the dark. The camp was a mixture of traditional humpies, ex-military tents and corrugated-iron shacks, and appeared to house about sixty people, mostly very old and very young. The kids scrambled to the car to greet Terry enthusiastically and the dogs barking in the camp woke up the dogs in the ute. The older women had a fire going ready for the kangaroo.

While it was cooking, Terry and I took a walk into the night with tin mugs of sweet black tea, which was the strongest thing allowed in the camp by the elders. He talked a lot about his plans: the old men and women passing on their knowledge and stories and dances to the young, while Terry and some of the others videotaped and recorded what they could.

The major problem was that Aboriginal beliefs meant that many of the women's dances were forbidden to the men and vice versa and, broadly put, once someone had died you weren't supposed to look at an image or literal representation of them. With the innovative problem-solving skills that had made him a force in advertising, Terry had called in some favours from a major effects production company. They'd produced a computer program that allowed him to create three-dimensional images of computer-generated figures that showed every movement and step of a dance, viewable from multiple angles. It was an ingenious marriage of modern electronics with an ancient culture.

'I guess this means you won't be going back to advertising any time soon?' I said.

He smiled. 'You play chess?'

I shook my head.

'Raymond Chandler once said, "Chess is as elaborate a waste of human intelligence as you can find outside of an advertising agency".'

'Sounds about right.'

'I play chess,' he said. 'Chandler was only half right.'

Away from the campfires, the night was pitch-black, apart from the carpet of stars and the yellow glow of the Springs on the distant horizon.

'Lot of light for twenty blokes. Must be scared of the dark,' Terry said wryly.

'Closer to three hundred,' I said.

'Maybe once,' he agreed, 'but not any more.'

Then we walked back to eat the kangaroo.

During the meal there was a flurry of activity on the outskirts of the camp.

'You've lucked out tonight, mate,' Terry said, chewing on a piece of charred macropod thigh. 'Dinner *and* a show. You could almost be in Las Vegas.'

The throaty drone of a didgeridoo and then the rhythmic beating of clap sticks put that image to bed pretty quickly. A group of young boys who I'd last seen in dusty stubbies and singlets pranced into the firelight in red loincloths, their bodies and faces decorated with white paint. They moved in a jumping gait, heavy footfalls lifting swirls of red dust up into the flickering firelight. As they danced I figured out that some were hunters and some were their prey. Terry gestured towards one who looked to be about ten or eleven and who was eerily successful in his role as a kangaroo.

'Tim,' he grinned. 'He's a real tearaway. Pain in the arse most of the time but he does a mean 'roo.'

'Not much he can get up to out here though, is there?' I asked.

'Don't you believe it,' Terry said, shaking his head. 'He hangs out with Ginger Meggs over there and if there's trouble to be had those two'll find it.'

The Ginger Meggs indicated was a pale-skinned, freckle-faced, red-headed ten-year-old who was sitting with a group of younger children, watching the dancing.

'Name is Gerald but everyone calls him Meggsie. His old man runs the cattle on Bitter Springs Station, which was a lot bigger before the Yanks carved off their slice for the base,' Terry explained. 'Kid heads out here whenever he gets the chance.'

When the dance ended we walked over to where the two boys were sitting together on the bonnet of a Land Cruiser, frantically stabbing at the buttons on their Gameboys.

'Hey, roughnut,' Terry said to Meggsie, 'your dad know where you are?'

Meggsie nodded without looking up from the screen. 'He said it was okay for me to stay the night.'

'You back in his good books then?'

The boy nodded.

'Little buggers broke into the Springs a couple of weeks back,' Terry said. 'Reckoned they wanted to see the dogs. Place is supposed to have a bunch of German Shepherds and Rottweilers. They found a hole under the outer fence where there was a washout in one of the gullies.'

'Sounds a bit dangerous,' I said. 'Those dogs are trained to bite hard and hang on tight.'

'Piece of piss,' Tim said, also without looking up from his Gameboy. 'No dogs anyway, just a crappy recording hooked up to some loudspeakers.'

'They might have been chained up in their kennels,' I suggested.

Tim shook his head dismissively. 'We looked in the kennels. No dogs and no dogshit.'

'What about the guards?'

'There's only a couple and they mostly look like they're drunk. We just kept out of their way. It wasn't hard.'

'And the robots don't care where you go,' Meggsie added.

'Robots?' I asked.

'The robots do all the work,' Tim said. 'They're always going some place.'

What the hell was going on? All my questions just produced more questions. And *robots*?

Terry and I walked back towards the main campfire. 'You think they're telling the truth?' I asked.

Terry shrugged. 'They're kids, who knows? Robots and invisible dogs. But they did come back with a bagful of Snickers they reckon they nicked from the canteen and our nearest corner shop is about a ten-hour drive.'

I looked back towards the two boys perched on the nose of the four-wheel drive.

'Bloody Meggsie,' Terry said. 'All he needs is a hat with corks and a face full of lamington. Ever seen anyone look more Australian?'

I glanced towards the campfire where a group of women and girls were dancing to the beat of clap sticks.

Terry grinned. 'Right,' he said. 'Point taken.'

THIRTY-TWO

Sleeping under a threadbare blanket next to the fire was surprisingly easy. When I woke up I could see Terry talking to a group of the older men. He broke off his conversation when he saw me stirring and wandered over.

'Morning. Sleep well?' he asked.

'Like a baby,' I said. 'Must be the desert air.'

He nodded. 'Hope you're not too hungry,' he said. 'We usually just make do with a dingo's breakfast out here.'

I looked at him quizzically.

'A piss and a good look around,' he said, smiling.

He saw my disappointment and laughed. 'The kids have cereal and you're welcome to that but the milk's powdered and the bore water doesn't improve the flavour. How about some damper and hot tea?'

I could live with that.

We squatted by the fire and sipped our tea.

'You haven't asked me what I'm doing out here,' I said.

Terry shrugged. 'Okay,' he said after a while, 'what are you doing out here?'

'I really can't say,' I said. 'I guess I was just commenting on your lack of inquisitiveness.'

'I figured if you were going to tell me you'd tell me.'

'Fair enough.'

This was about as close to having a heart-to-heart as two Aussie blokes were ever likely to come.

'How'd you feel about young Tim showing me how he got into the Springs?' I asked.

Terry shook his head. 'That place isn't healthy.'

'I just want the entry point for reference. We'll go straight there and come straight back.'

'What if there's trouble?'

'I try to avoid trouble wherever possible.' This was true but just lately trouble was having no problem finding me.

'So that gun in your pocket's just for avoiding trouble, then?'

I nodded. 'It *is* important.'

'Straight there and straight back?'

'You got it. Straight there and straight back.'

Terry stood up. 'Only if Tim says yes, though. But it's not like I'd expect the little bugger to say anything else.'

We walked over to where Tim and Meggsie were having breakfast.

'You two feel like showing me where you went under the wire?' I asked.

Tim looked expectantly towards Terry, who gave a small nod. 'Take plenty of water and see what you can pick up for lunch,' Terry said. Tim grinned and the two boys raced off to get ready.

'You take good care of those boys, okay? The Springs is a bad place.'

'Since the Yanks moved in, you mean?'

He shook his head. 'Long time before that. A long, long time.' He had a look on his face that I figured maybe Grace would understand. I remembered when *Adnews* had described Terry as a young man with both eyes on the future, but right now I had the feeling he was looking backwards about forty thousand years.

It was still crisp when we set off but by the time we were closing in on the base the sun was well up and the heat of the day set up a shimmer on the horizon. Meggsie and I were both wearing shirts, jeans and boots, and Meggsie had a broad-brimmed straw hat protecting his fair skin. Terry had loaned me a battered Akubra and I was carrying a backpack with six two-litre plastic bottles of bore water. Tim was wearing a pair of St Kilda footy shorts about two sizes too big for him and carrying a short spear and a woomera. He wandered ahead barefoot across the scorching sand. Meggsie kept pretty much to my side.

'Tim's a really good tracker,' Meggsie said after about an hour of silence. 'The old men take him out sometimes, when they go after kangaroo. They reckon he knows how the 'roos think.'

Tim made a small gesture with his right hand and Meggsie steered me to the right, away from a rocky outcrop.

'Snake, probably,' he said. 'Terry reckons we have to bring you back in one piece.'

Great, I now had two ten-year-old bodyguards.

After another hundred yards or so, Tim stopped. Meggsie put up his hand and we both halted. Tim didn't move for a full two minutes and then he casually fitted the end of his spear into the woomera. The spear rested shoulder-high for another thirty seconds and then it was on its way with Tim and Meggsie racing in pursuit, whooping like the two pre-adolescent boys they were. When I caught up with them they were standing over a large goanna, pinned to the ground by the spear through its body. The long claws on the lizard's feet were scraping feebly at the sand in an attempt to break free. Tim casually picked up a rock and smashed it down on the creature's head. He pulled the spear free, wiped its point in the sand and grinned. 'Not exactly Macca's but she'll do, eh?'

Meggsie shook his head. 'I don't like goanna much,' he said, then looked at me. 'You ever been to Macca's? Tim reckons the chips are unreal.'

'French fries,' Tim said. He picked up his spear and woomera and grabbed the limp goanna by the tail.

'They do do a good chip,' I said. 'You haven't ever been to the big smoke?'

Meggsie shook his head. 'Not since I was two. But Dad reckons maybe this Christmas we might go to Adelaide to see my nanna. She'll take me to Macca's, I reckon.'

The look of expectation on his face made me laugh out loud. 'Listen mate, if we can find some spuds and oil back at the camp what say we have a go at making our own French fries? To go with our goanna burgers.'

They seemed to find the concept of goanna burgers hysterically funny. Tim started skipping across the sand singing, 'Two all goanna patties, special sauce, lettuce, cheese, pickles, onions on a sesame seed bun.'

Meggsie had a turn, but he sang, 'Two all goanna patties, special sauce, lettuce, cheese, pickles, onions on a sesame seed BUM!'

The two boys started running in circles, laughing and yelling 'BUM! BUM! BUM!' up at the blue sky.

They were right, it *was* funny. That's part of what being ten is all about.

When the hysteria subsided we continued on our trek, proceeding past several DO NOT PROCEED PAST THIS POINT signs without attracting any choppers from the base. The outer-perimeter barbed-wire fence appeared after another half an hour. Tim led me down to the creek bed and along to the place where they had wriggled their way under the wire and into the base. The gap looked tight but I decided I could probably make it. Then I noticed some fresh tyre tracks up on the ridge inside the wire.

'You two really get in and out without being spotted?' I asked.

Meggsie looked at Tim. Both boys looked at the ground.

'They chased us,' Tim said eventually, 'but you can't tell Terry.'

'Show him your bum,' Meggsie said.

'Got sesame seeds on it, does it?' I asked, and Meggsie gave me a severe look that said this was no laughing matter.

Tim pulled down his shorts and revealed a jagged rip in the skin of his left buttock. The scab looked about ready to fall off.

I could see a small piece of fading fabric caught on one of the lower barbs of the wire fence. There'd probably be a dried-up piece of Tim's bum cheek attached to it.

'If Terry found out they shot at us he'd get really mad,' Tim said. 'You can't tell him, okay? He might do something that'd get him into trouble.'

What kind of sick bastards would start shooting at a couple of ten-year-old kids? I'd be quite happy to join Terry in kicking in the front door of the base and asking. Then I saw it, just beyond the fence.

'Promise you won't tell Terry, all right?' Tim pleaded. He tugged at my sleeve to get my attention.

'Okay,' I said, 'but first you two have to promise *me* something. Promise me you won't go back under that wire. Ever.'

'Me and Tim aren't afraid,' Meggsie said. 'Are we, Tim?'

I took them closer to the perimeter fence and made them

lie down on the sand. 'Look just beyond the wire,' I said, 'a smidge past that tree root.'

The three thin metal spikes stuck out just a few centimetres above the sand. I pointed out a second trio of spikes about a metre to the right.

'What are they?' Tim asked.

'Land mines. They must have planted them when they found out how you got into the base.'

'Are they dangerous?' Meggsie asked.

'Mate,' I said, 'if you step on those spikes or even just brush past them, there'll be one hell of a big bang and you'll wind up in tiny pieces all over the wire.'

The two boys were silent for a long time.

'But we could fit between 'em, no worries,' Tim said.

Meggsie nodded. 'Piece of piss.'

'That's what you're supposed to think,' I said. 'See that little indentation in the sand, right in the middle?'

Tim got it straightaway but he had to point it out to Meggsie, who finally made out the slight dip.

'You walk carefully between the two mines you can see and step on the one hidden in the middle. Probably a Jumping Jack.'

'No shit?' Tim said. It wasn't an appropriate time to have a go at his language.

'What's a Jumping Jack?' Meggsie asked.

'Antipersonnel mine,' I explained. 'They killed a hell of a lot of people in Vietnam.'

The two boys looked at me blankly.

'You've heard of the Vietnam War?' I asked.

Meggsie shook his head.

'Is it like the one in Iraq?' Tim said.

'Pretty much,' I said. 'Anyway, in Vietnam the American soldiers called Jumping Jacks "step-and-a-halfs". You stand on one and get about a step-and-a-half further when it shoots up to waist height and goes off. Ka-boom! Same result as the other ones though, little bits of you two plastered all over the landscape.'

It was a long, slow walk back to camp as Tim and Meggsie carefully checked out every bit of sand before they put their foot on it. I was fairly certain I'd frightened them off going back under that wire any time soon. Trouble was I wasn't sure that *I* had any alternative if I was going to find out what was going on at the base.

THIRTY-THREE

We made it back to camp just on lunchtime and found Terry and a small group gathered around a cool-looking trail bike.

It was the military version of the Yamaha XT600, with beefed-up suspension, long-range fuel tanks and gun racks. Even rigged for quiet running, it could hit over one-fifty on the flat and the extra fuel gave it a range of about three hundred k's. Under the layer of dust it was painted the same colour as the desert sand and it was loaded down with equipment which I recognised as army issue.

Tim and Meggsie sprinted ahead as soon as they saw the bike and Terry picked Tim up and dropped him onto the seat.

'Hey Alby, come and meet my cuz Jimmy!'

Jimmy was wearing desert camouflage fatigues, the new pattern, softened with a layer of dust and worn down by hard work. He had a long piece of khaki camouflage netting draped round his neck as a scarf, along with his motorcycle goggles. Brown combat boots completed the outfit.

The orange and green Double Diamond colour patch on his shoulder indicated he was in Norforce, the North West Mobile Force which was one of the Australian Army's three Regional Force Surveillance Units. These units patrol the top of Australia looking for illegal entry, drugs and just generally keeping an eye on things. There were a lot of Aboriginals in Norforce. It made sense since the area was their backyard. It was a hell of a big backyard and they ran patrols on trail bikes and in specially fitted-out Land Rovers.

Norforce were a bit like the Long Range Desert Group in North Africa in World War II. The LRDG soldiers, initially all Kiwi volunteers, were tough, self-reliant men. They disappeared behind enemy lines for weeks at a time, spying on German and Italian troop movements or suddenly appearing out of the trackless desert to blow up fuel and ammunition dumps with improvised incendiary bombs or to roar down the runways of enemy airfields, blazing away at parked fighters and bombers with the multiple machine guns mounted on their customised Ford F30 and Chevrolet trucks.

Jimmy here looked like he'd be right at home on the back of a speeding Chevy, blazing away with twin Vickers K guns or hurling Lewes bombs onto the wings of Stukas and Heinkels. He had a collapsible stock M4 carbine slung casually over one shoulder, muzzle down. It was the special-ops modified version with a Day Scope and the shortened, quick-release M203 grenade launcher mounted under the barrel.

'Bit unfair on the 'roos, isn't it?' I said, indicating the carbine as we shook hands.

He shrugged. 'If I use the grenade launcher they wind up in chunks the right size for kebabs.'

I smiled at the joke but Tim and Meggsie fell about laughing. I heard a half-whispered comment about kebabs on a bum.

'Thought you guys used Steyers?' I said. I was just doing a bit of digging. The standard-issue weapon for Norforce, like the rest of the army, was the Austeyer, a locally built version of the 5.56mm Austrian Styer bullpup design assault rifle. It was odd that the Yanks issued M16s and the newer M4s to regular troops and the Steyers to special ops while we did exactly the opposite.

'We're doing an evaluation on the M4,' Jimmy said. 'Seeing how it holds up in the desert.'

I was going to suggest he could just ask the SAS since they'd had a fair bit of experience with the weapon in Iraq but I decided against it.

'So what brings you out this way?' he asked.

'Sightseeing.'

'Me too. Not thinking about sightseeing out that way, are you?' He pointed his thumb back over his shoulder in the direction of the Springs.

'Tourist brochure said they do a mean Devonshire tea,' I said.

Jimmy laughed. 'Not the healthiest destination in the world. The Springs, I mean. Bloke with any sense would steer clear of the place.' His tone told me it was more than a suggestion. He walked over to the trail bike and took a Kevlar combat helmet from the handlebars. 'Keep in touch, Terry, eh,' he said as he put the helmet on.

I assumed that one of the large panniers on the side of the bike held a Raven high-frequency radio and his dropping by for a chat was no coincidence. Jimmy's NORFORCE shoulder patch was newly sewn on and barely covered by dust. I was fairly sure there was a lot more to cousin Jimmy than met the eye. He looked at me and I knew he knew what I was thinking. He definitely had me pegged as a bloke without any sense.

'You should have a bit of a chinwag with the old men,' he said. 'They've got some very interesting stories.' He lifted a reluctant Tim off the bike and then straddled it, kicking the warm engine into life with one sharp downward thrust of his leg. He pulled the goggles up over his eyes, waved, and took off in a cloud of dust.

After my little chat with Meggsie and Tim last night and our stroll this morning that was all that I needed – more interesting stories.

Meggsie found a plastic container of canola oil, some bruised-looking potatoes and a blackened frying-pan and we had a go at making chips. Tim announced that Macca's had nothing to fear from me but I noticed he had his eye on Meggsie's chips when he finished his own. After lunch Terry and one of the elders led me on the long trek through the dunes back to the bitumen road. We found a tiny spot of shade on the side of a sandhill and looked down on the black ribbon snaking its way through the empty desert towards the white domes in the distance.

We sat in silence for a while, just watching. I figured the older man would tell me what he had to tell me when he was ready, so I waited. He began speaking softly in a language that I imagined went back to the Dreamtime, and he spoke for a long time, pausing occasionally to point out something on the ribbon of asphalt and then making symbols on the sand. Terry listened attentively, nodding, then told me the old man's story.

The road had been built before the base, some twenty-five years ago. When the road was ready and the old RAAF runway had been repaired and extended the planes began arriving – C-17 Globemasters, from the old man's description. C-17s use blown flaps, vortex generators and thrust reversers on landing so their short field performance is excellent. Plus they're manoeuvrable enough to do a neat three-point turn so the strip at Larunga would have been a doddle.

First the transport planes brought in trucks and heavy construction equipment and then building materials and pre-fabricated housing for a temporary base camp at the airfield.

More prefabricated housing arrived for the spy base construction crews and then all the materials and equipment needed to build a modern satellite surveillance facility began flooding in.

Day and night for months the trucks shuttled from the airfield to the construction site in convoys of ten to twenty vehicles. Terry translated as the old man explained how the road had worn unevenly. Less on the right, where the empty left-hand-drive trucks hurtled through the day and the night towards the landing strip. Heavily laden, the trucks then lumbered back in the left-hand lane, the weight of their cargo tearing up the bitumen so that road crews were constantly patching the surface of the roadway.

There were accidents, of course, with such heavy traffic and after one incident some of the younger men from the tribe had examined the crashed truck. Abandoned by its crew and waiting for a recovery vehicle from the base, the truck carried pallets from the transport planes. The heavy pallets, loaded by forklift at the airfield, held bags of cement and gravel for concrete making. And sand. Bags of sand. These guys were flying sand halfway round the world to make concrete in the middle of the largest sandy desert on the continent.

The sun was higher in the sky now and our patch of shade was disappearing quickly. I wanted a closer look at the road so we moved slowly down the side of a dune to the edge of the asphalt strip. There were abandoned blackened and rusting barrels scattered beside the roadway where patching of the surface had taken place.

The old men, used to studying the birds that flew over the arid land, had been watching the Globemasters. During the early building period, the huge aircraft, heavily laden with cargo, ponderously thumped down on the runway, engines thundering in reverse thrust as they fought to stop the momentum before the end of the airstrip.

When the building work was finally completed, the old man explained, the Globemaster visits dropped to two or three a month. The trucks then began running in fives and sixes to collect food and fuel for the base and to transport incoming or outgoing personnel. It had continued like that for many years, the road repair crews only needing to make sporadic visits with their drums of tar.

But then, a few years back, the Globemaster arrivals suddenly became much more frequent again and the trucks, usually running empty from the base out to the airfield, had begun tearing up the right-hand side of the road. There were more trucks too, a lot more, and for the next few months the road patching crews had been out constantly, sometimes seven days a week.

And the Globemasters were landing easily and taxiing quickly to the cargo-loading areas. From a distance the old men had watched as supposedly empty trucks from the base lumbered up to the planes and afterwards the huge transporters would take the whole length of the runway to struggle clear of the ground.

Once one had failed to make it, crashing and burning in

the spinifex, three miles from the runway. Some of Terry's mob had picked through the smouldering wreckage before being driven off by warning gunfire from the base security people. Every inch of the cargo space on the plane had been crammed with computers and sophisticated electronic equipment. All burned up in the fire, of course.

After a few months this flurry of activity subsided and the Globemaster arrivals dropped back to two a month. The truck convoys were down to five or six vehicles again and they went out to the airfield empty and came back loaded. Business as usual.

The old man spoke to Terry, who looked up the road in the direction of the base. 'Company,' he said and we tumbled into a gully as the roar of engines carried over the afternoon stillness. Six trucks – US Army five-tonners in olive drab – roared past us, dust billowing in their wake.

A shadow flashed over us and when I looked up I could see the plane about a thousand feet above us banking slowly for a straight-in approach to the runway.

The old man spoke to Terry.

'The planes don't have markings any more,' Terry said. 'They used to have numbers, now they're just grey.'

The old man was right. Air Force grey and from what I could see no numbers or markings.

Jesus, what a bastard. I knew where all the answers were going to be. I also knew I was getting too bloody old to start climbing over security fences.

THIRTY-FOUR

Getting into the base was easier than I had expected. Getting *into* trouble always is. Terry and some of the men from the camp pushed a wreck of an abandoned four-wheel drive up to the road and parked it slewed across the ribbon of asphalt with the hood up. We shook hands and they set off back to the camp. Having them out of the way seemed like a good idea.

I waited in the gully to the left of the road and heard the Globemaster roaring off the runway about half an hour before the trucks arrived on their return journey. As I had hoped, they pulled up short of the abandoned vehicle, the last truck in the convoy about level with my hiding place.

The drivers climbed down and gathered around the first truck. All the men carried M16 rifles, which was the only military thing about them. Headgear was an assortment of baseball caps, soft jungle hats and headbands. The rest of the outfit was Raybans, T-shirts, singlets, combat pants or shorts and boots. They must have had a very hip commanding officer.

One of the group spotted Terry's mob through his binoculars. He muttered some obscenities, swung his rifle up and emptied the magazine into the abandoned four-wheel drive. With whoops and yells the others followed suit and under cover of the din I was able to sprint up to the tailgate of the last truck and haul myself aboard.

The drivers climbed back into their vehicles and the lead truck pushed the bullet-riddled hulk off the road and started the convoy on its way back to the base. It was hot under the canvas cover and the swaying and bumping made it dangerous to do anything but lie flat amongst the crates that made up the cargo. There were only six, barely enough of a load to make the trip worthwhile. One of the crates had a corner smashed in, probably from bad handling, so I gave in to curiosity and gently eased off the lid. Surprise, surprise! I was keeping company with a load of Czech-made semi-automatic pistols. Very curious. They were a cheap and nasty little gun and not the sort of weapon any self-respecting security guard at a satellite spy station would carry. Last time I'd seen a gun like this it had been pointing right between my eyes at a highway truckstop.

We scorched through the gate and into the main compound area. The road snaked past several low buildings, one of which was marked 'Cafeteria' and then the trucks slowed, circled, and slowly backed up against a windowless warehouse structure of dull aluminium. They stopped with their tailgates close to the wall. The drivers climbed down and drifted off and I overheard mutterings about lunch and coffee and someone complaining about soggy microwaved fried chicken.

After deciding enough time had passed, I slipped over the tailgate and got my bearings. The middle of the compound held the giant silver dome that concealed the 'Big Ear' radio dish. Two smaller domes to its right were for re-transmitting dishes, I guessed. There were a dozen or so other low-rise structures, which had to be the offices and recreation and dormitory areas. The computers would be underground in hardened shelters.

Someone turned the corner and I spun round to see if they were armed and if I should make a run for it. I squinted into the afternoon light at the two figures silhouetted at the corner. They stood for a moment and then came towards me. But they didn't walk, they glided with a soft electrical hum. Two dummies, about my size, in US Air Force uniforms, travelling on some sort of hidden track. What the hell was going on? More movement came from the cafeteria. A dozen dummies glided out of a doorway and split up into twos and threes, going off in different directions. Occasionally two coming from opposite ends of the compound would stop face-to-face for a moment and then continue on their way. These must have been Tim's robots. It was like visiting Santa's Magic Cave at Myer's Toyland at Christmas when I was a kid.

Unfortunately the spectacle had me so transfixed that I missed someone coming out of the cafeteria who wasn't a dummy. Or Santa Claus for that matter. He was yelling and unslinging his rifle so I sprinted for the nearest open doorway, which was the warehouse.

When my eyes became accustomed to the lower light level the Christmas Cave feeling came back. The place was stacked to the roof with containers and shipping crates. A lot of them had been opened and the contents were strewn haphazardly around the warehouse. My first impression was that it wasn't exactly the kind of stuff you needed to run a high-tech Star Wars satellite base. I could see a lot of guns and a lot of ammo. Tons of the stuff. There were sealed plastic bags of white powder stacked up on steel shelving. The bags had Chinese characters printed on them and, given a choice between guessing they held heroin or self-raising flour, I knew which way I'd lean. And there were large bales of what looked like grass. The stuff you smoke, not the stuff you mow. They had so much of it that someone had set up a target range down one side of the warehouse with bullseyes pinned to the bales.

On a gunsmith's bench was a neatly cleaned 9mm Walther PK-S submachine gun, which I grabbed along with half-a-dozen magazines. The Walther had a sling attached so I hung it around my neck. There was a lot of noise outside now but I didn't expect much shooting due to the fact that I was literally sitting on a powder keg.

THIRTY-FIVE

The voice coming through the doorway was familiar. It was Sheldon. He wanted to come in and talk. That was okay by me. My hiding spot between some crates seemed safe enough so I agreed.

'You are one tough son of a gun, Alby boy,' Sheldon said as he stepped through the door.

He was wearing an open flak vest over his shirt and carrying a Swedish K. Good to see some people held with tradition, even in the CIA. He stopped just inside the doorway, which was quite far enough as far as I was concerned.

'Now we got us a situation here which we need to sort out PDQ,' he said as he lit a cigarette. Sheldon pronounced it 'sit-chay-shun' in a sort of down-home folksy way that might have been charming if I didn't already know his solution to this particular 'sit-chay-shun' would involve me getting shot full of holes.

'You have any suggestions?' I yelled. 'And don't come any closer.'

The noise of the bolt as I cocked the Walther made him stiffen a little.

'Well,' Sheldon drawled, 'I could radio that big old plane to come on back and we could send you off to some place sunny with enough of the foldin' green to see out your days in style and comfort.'

'I'm not so keen on flying these days, Sheldon.'

'Understandable, buddy boy. Understandable.'

It might have been my imagination but Sheldon's accent seemed to be getting more and more southern by the moment. If this discussion went on much longer he'd wind up sounding like Foghorn Leghorn. And just as I was thinking about dumb cartoon characters Gordon Dalkeith walked in.

Gordon was wearing a very silly-looking safari suit but the Uzi machine pistol hanging off his shoulder wasn't all that amusing. Or maybe it was. With Sheldon the effect was a bit scary but on Gordon it looked like a big kid playing dress-ups. Sort of 'Bags I'm the Superspy'.

But now I knew exactly whose side Gordon was on. Not mine.

'What the hell's going on, Gordon?' I yelled. 'What are you and Sheldon playing at?'

'Oh, it's not a game, buddy boy,' Sheldon drawled. 'Gordon and I have worked out our own little free-trade agreement.'

'I'm very happy for you both, but what's that got to do with Harry and me?'

'When you and Wardell stumbled on this operation you must have known you'd become a liability,' Gordon said.

'To tell you the truth, Gordon, I've got no idea what you're talking about. Harry was doing the Springs vetting all by himself.'

'Sorry, buddy boy, that's all academic now,' Sheldon said.

'Humour me. If you're going to rub me out, at least tell me what's going on.' I was stalling for time while I desperately tried to figure out an escape route.

Gordon looked across at Sheldon, who shrugged and started talking.

'Well Alby, you see, in the mid-eighties when the old Soviet Union looked like it was about ready to start falling apart and the Cold War was on its last legs they reassessed all of our intelligence assets and Bitter Springs turned out to be less important than we'd figured.'

Sheldon explained that the equipment at the base was ready for an expensive upgrading and the recent development of nano-satellites had stopped that being a worthwhile proposition.

Nano-satellites, tiny and almost impossible-to-detect surveillance devices about the size of a domestic rubbish bin, had been chucked out of the space shuttle from its very first mission and were now orbiting the earth in vast numbers. The encrypted data they collected could be downlinked through hub stations disguised as commercial weather satellites and that had totally revolutionised the way electronic eavesdropping was now done. The US still made a big show of putting up regular giant spy satellites every so often but it was all a diversion. Just like the Springs, which wasn't really needed any more.

'It was Sheldon who came up with the idea of making it look like the base was still fully functional,' Gordon added.

Of course it would have been. Sheldon's rat cunning knew no bounds. Why totally abandon the base when it could still serve a purpose as a deterrent? It was a masterstroke of deception and probably what had earned Sheldon his promotion and a reward of a cushy posting down-under.

Gordon proudly explained how the increased activity of the Globemasters hauling away everything of strategic value from the base had been carefully spun through the press into a purported massive upgrade of the facility. They made it appear that the Springs was even more capable of spying on enemies of the US and controlling retaliation for any nuclear first strike.

Soviet and Chinese photo recon satellites wouldn't have been able to discern that the planes were taking stuff away rather than delivering new equipment. That also explained the dummies on the tracks. The photo reconnaissance satellites would have recorded an apparently fully staffed base. The robots no doubt emitted low-level infra-red energy as well so the night passes would show heat tracks of people still working round the clock. Ingenious, really.

No longer needed, and gutted of all its hardware, Bitter Springs was just an empty shell sitting smack bang in the middle of the wide brown land, acting as both a threat and a decoy, and waiting to suck in any first strike. What a pisser!

'And the two cargo flights a month were kept up for cover, right?'

'Well, we had to make it look like it was business as usual,' Gordon said.

I could see that two almost empty Globemasters flying in and out of the country every month just to keep up the charade of a fully operational base would have become very tempting to someone like Sheldon Asher. And to his new best buddies in the Sydney underworld. All that cargo space and no customs, no immigration, no quarantine, no bugger-all.

With all the brownie points he'd have earned with his plan to extend the useful life of the base it must have been easy for Sheldon to sell the CIA and the US Defence Department on the logic of contracting a private company to maintain the base and operate those flights. Good from the security angle and, more importantly, good for the bottom line. All the usual bullshit. A deft double shuffle through the books to get three Globemasters moved sideways out of the AMC and bingo! – it's Air America time all over again.

So with Gordon's connivance Sheldon had his own airstrip, his own private airline and a free pass to fly whatever he liked in and out of the country any time he felt like it. These bozos were hauling guns and drugs and God-only-knew what else around the South Pacific without a worry in the world. And using our country as a staging post.

'It was all done in the interest of national security, you know,' Gordon said.

That was always his rationalisation. I wondered who else knew. Probably no-one in our government. Yeah, right, who was I kidding?

'Doesn't sound too secure to me, Gordon,' I shouted back. 'Keeping us as a nuclear target for no reason?'

It wasn't really for no reason of course. Even today every Soviet or Chinese ICBM aimed at central Australia was one less aimed at the good old US of A.

I'm not much of a flag waver at the best of times but Gordon and Sheldon perverting our security for personal gain and bumping off anyone who got in the way was really starting to get on my wick. Getting a bullet through my left shoulder really got my dander up.

The impact spun me around and into the side of a crate. There was an intense burning pain in my shoulder but I managed to fire off half a magazine in the direction of the sniper, mostly by instinct I guess. A shriek and a thud seemed to indicate a lucky hit. Gordon emptied his Uzi magazine in a wildly inaccurate arc and fled the warehouse. Sheldon had backed off moments before the shot. That was why the two of them were happy to keep yapping away. They were stalling to give the shooter time to work his way into position.

My fall against the crates had knocked one to the ground and its contents lay scattered around my feet – cylindrical containers, smoke markers. I dropped a couple into my jacket pocket and began arming and throwing the rest towards the door. Not easy with only one arm. White smoke started to fill the warehouse. Crouching and running got me over to the shooting range. While I could still see I grabbed at anything with a sling. One grab got me a grenade launcher, which I broke open. It held a parachute flare cartridge so I snapped it shut, cocked it and fired the shell into the bales of marijuana. I hoped I was far enough back for the shell to arm itself. There was a *pop* and a bright light began to flicker from the centre of the bales. Bingo! The bales started to smoke and I knew it was time to make a move. In another ten minutes anyone inside this building would start working up to a serious case of the munchies.

Through the haze I could just make out a group of the decoy dummies moving past me on their tracks. I began hanging weapons around their necks and watched as they glided out through the warehouse door. The distraction worked and there was suddenly a lot of gunfire with very few bullets coming my way.

What did come my way next was a big Hummer. It came out of the smoke at the doorway and I emptied the rest of my magazine into the windscreen. The driver lost control and smashed through the rear wall of the warehouse. This looked like a sensible way out for me too. Especially as the bales of dope were building up into quite a healthy conflagration.

My shoulder was getting numb now but I still managed to change the magazine on the Walther one-handed. The sling helped me keep the muzzle up as I headed through the smoke-filled compound towards the big dome. A figure came out of the haze and I fired off a quick burst and kept going.

It was eerie inside the huge structure – hundreds of feet high and completely empty, the giant antennae long since dismantled and shipped away. Across the floor was the room I wanted – Base Security. I set off my last two smoke bombs in the middle of the dome. The security office door was locked so I shot my way in, like in the movies. The emergency phone was red and it still worked. Another part of the cover. Someone probably checked in with Darwin once or twice a day to maintain the pretence that the big dish was still on high alert.

The phone was ringing somewhere and it kept on ringing. It rang fifteen or twenty times before a bored voice answered with 'Rapid Response'.

'Yeah, mate,' I snarled, 'real rapid. Get your arse in gear. There's a terrorist attack happening at the Springs satellite installation.'

There was a long pause, then the voice said, 'Struth', then, 'Jesus, are you pulling my leg?'

At that moment the smoke in the dome set off the base fire-detection klaxons, the sprinkler system kicked in and a Hummer smashed through the dome's main doors with a top-mounted .50 calibre heavy machine gun firing long bursts in every direction.

'Does this sound like a drill?' I screamed. 'Pull your finger out and get airborne.'

The office window shattered behind me and the stream of bullets blew the security switchboard to pieces. The phone went dead in my hand but this was a plus. A dead phone line should confirm to the Rapid Response commander that something wasn't right. He'd have no other option than to send up the Blackhawk helicopters with their on-duty commando teams. That was, of course, assuming they weren't out in their zodiacs fishing for barramundi.

I fired off a couple of quick bursts towards the sound of the Hummer engine. A long burst of fire came back and then the sound of the vehicle leaving the way it had come in. Help was on the way. All I had to do was stay alive until it arrived. Someone carrying a gun came out on my right. A short burst got it in the chest and it toppled awkwardly – one of the dummies.

There were other figures visible through the smoke now. They were forming a ragged skirmish line and it looked like they'd be coming my way before too long. Even if the Blackhawks were airborne already they were still a long way off. The magazine on the Walther was almost empty and I only had one more. This was starting to look like a less than ideal situation.

The Hummer came back through the smoke and lined up for a direct run on the office. I pointed the Walther in the general direction of the vehicle, which suddenly exploded. It might have been a lucky shot, but it wasn't, because I hadn't pulled the trigger. The Hummer flipped over on its nose and the gunner and driver were flung out of their seats before it toppled back onto its wheels and started to burn. I could hear more engines outside now but the note was different. Then there was firing – short, disciplined bursts, not the cowboy sprays of Sheldon's private army, who were pulling back now towards the main doorway in total disarray.

I needed to get out too. The sprinklers were having no effect on the burning Hummer and when the vehicle's fifty cal ammunition started cooking off it would get very uncomfortable in here very fast. There was a master switch on the wall which killed the alarm sirens. The firing outside seemed to have stopped and I could hear someone issuing orders.

'Thank Christ for some peace and quiet,' a voice said behind me. I spun around and tried to aim the Walter one-handed.

'I'll get our medic to have a look at that arm,' Jimmy said. 'Told you this bloody place wasn't healthy.'

THIRTY-SIX

The dull thud of exploding grenades was coming from the rapidly growing inferno of the warehouse buildings. The crates of small-arms ammunition would be next, popping off like strings of New Year's firecrackers in Chinatown. The sprinklers in the warehouse wouldn't make any headway against a blaze like that.

There were half-a-dozen Land Rovers parked in a semi-circle outside the dome. One still had strands of razor wire festooned over its bull-bar from smashing its way in through the perimeter fences. Another, a six-wheel-drive Perenti model, mounted a Milan anti-tank rocket launcher, which explained what had happened to the Hummer in the dome.

Norforce troopers were efficiently stripping Sheldon's private army of their weapons and equipment and fastening their hands behind their backs with plastic ties.

The unit medic gave my shoulder a quick once-over and

slapped a field dressing on it. 'Straight through,' he said. 'Missed the bone. You'll live.' He smiled. 'Gunna hurt like a bastard soon, though.'

He moved off towards half-a-dozen figures lying on the ground. They were mostly minor wounds too, apart from the pair blown out of the Hummer by the anti-tank missile. And Sheldon. It looked like old Shit for Brains had drawled his last drawl. There was a United States Marine Corps major in full battle dress standing over the body.

'Heart attack,' the major said.

I nodded. It sounded feasible. Getting shot in the chest with a full magazine from an M4 could tend to slow down the old ticker. And of course a coroner's certificate reading 'Death by Natural Causes' would generate a lot less of a mess, politically speaking. Sheldon's missus back home would get an urn full of ashes and a civil service pension, and the CIA wouldn't have to embarrass themselves by putting his name up on the wall at Langley as having died in the line of duty. There would be a brief memorial service, with a nice eulogy from the assistant to the assistant to the assistant director, and the fight against the forces of darkness would go forward with one less stalwart soldier. It looked like one of Sheldon's famous win/win sit-chay-shuns. For everyone except Sheldon, of course.

I gave the Marine Corps major a kiss. No tongues naturally, since she was on duty.

'That serious?' Grace asked, indicating the dressing on my shoulder.

I shook my head. 'Just a flesh wound. I'll live.' Her uniform had a name tape sewn above the right pocket. It read MANKILLER. 'Nice uniform,' I said. 'Exactly how many different outfits do you work for?'

'Well, that would be classified, wouldn't it?' She slipped the M4 sling over her shoulder and smiled. 'And haven't you heard that a bit of mystery keeps the romance alive?'

'I've had it up to pussy's bow with the classified and the mysterious,' I said. 'I wouldn't mind the odd fact.'

'Change of administration in Washington means a change of policy,' she said. 'They wanted this situation tidied up when they found out about it. I help tidy things up.'

'And neatly done,' I said, glancing around the shattered and burning compound.

'Hey, don't look at *me*,' Grace said. 'You started it.'

A huge fireball blew out the roof of the closer warehouse and a rocket-propelled grenade whizzed out of the flames, cartwheeling through the air before exploding against the big dome. Flames started licking out over the skin of the structure. The next Russian photo recon satellite was going to pass over this afternoon and those photographs, downlinked to Moscow, were sure to cause a lot of discussion. But with what was going on in Russia right now would they really care?

Jimmy ambled across the compound towards us, his M4 slung loosely across his chest, muzzle down. The look was relaxed but I noticed his finger was resting carefully on the trigger guard. He took his hand off the weapon for a moment to casually salute Grace. She saluted back.

'Thanks for the heads-up, Jimmy.'

'No problem, Major,' he said. 'These Norforce boys are pretty good, eh.'

Grace nodded. 'They can cover my back any time.'

'We're packing up,' Jimmy went on. 'We wanna be long gone before anyone shows up.'

I looked around. The Norforce troopers were loading the prisoners and the dead and wounded into their Land Rovers.

'We'll sort out the details,' Grace said.

That was fine by me. She climbed into one of the Land Rovers and settled in comfortably behind the M60 machine gun. 'I might be in Sydney next week,' she said. 'Lunch? I know an excellent Italian place.'

'Sounds good,' I said, and then, 'Mankiller?'

She glanced down at the pocket patch. 'I needed a code-name for this operation. Wilma Mankiller was the first female chief of the Cherokee Nation and a bit of a hero of mine. It's definitely a name that makes people sit up and take notice.'

'It certainly got my attention,' I said.

'You need a ride anywhere?' Jimmy asked.

'Something I need to take care of here first,' I said.

He nodded. 'We'll saddle up, then.'

'Going to twirl your finger in the air to get them to start their engines?'

'You bet,' he grinned. 'One of the perks of command.'

'You're Special Air Service, right?' I asked.

'Bugger, don't tell me they left those dammed SAS number plates on the Land Rovers again.'

I laughed and shook my head. 'Just a wild guess.'

His eyes swept carefully across the compound, making sure everyone was accounted for.

'Nah, mate,' he said finally, 'none of our mob in the SAS.' He grinned. 'Not the kind of job we're good at.'

He winked, twirled his finger in the air and the vehicles fired up in unison. As the Land Rovers gunned their way back out through the broken wire I waved to Grace. What a lucky man I was. How many blokes have ever had a heavily armed United States Marine Corps major blow them a kiss?

At the rate the fires were spreading the cafeteria looked like the safest place to be so naturally that's where I found Gordon. He was sitting in the empty main dining area, drinking coffee out of a styrofoam cup. The coffee had that terrible powdery, non-dairy creamer stuff floating on it and some of the powder was on the corners of his mouth. Gordon's eyes were tired and vacant when he looked up at me. He wasn't really a fighter and the last few hours must have taken it out of him. His machine pistol was on the table with the magazine next to it. Out of ammo, out of luck and nearly out of time.

The Rapid Response Blackhawks would be coming in very soon. My plan was to be out in the open by the landing pad, down on my knees, hands way up high. These special-ops bods could sometimes get a bit twitchy, and anyone not waving the flag and singing the national anthem stood a very good chance of being shot full of holes. I sort of wished I had an autographed picture of the PM I could wave.

But what was I going to do with Gordon? That was the real problem. He'd had Harry killed – or he'd at least gone along with Sheldon on it – and then almost blown up an airliner full of Hong Kong–bound holiday-makers just to get me. There was also Graeme Rutherford in a coma and the injured street kid at the ATM. Plus the drug importation and the gun running which had led to how many deaths? On top of this was his connivance with a CIA plan that left the country sitting dumbly for all those years as a juicy nuclear target for no good reason at all.

I sat down at the next table and stared at him. He didn't look like what he was – a murderer for certain, and potentially a mass murderer. But then again, what does a murderer look like? There were more explosions outside, then a long loud rumble and the cafeteria building shook. It was probably the big dome caving in on itself.

'They'll make all this go away, you know,' Gordon said finally. 'I'll take my pension and retire to the country to breed springer spaniels and you'll be the ideal person to get my job. I could put in a good word for you, if you like.'

He was right, of course. This whole thing was way too embarrassing. There'd be a lot of heated phone calls between

Canberra and Washington and then a cover story would be released. Later a slightly more intriguing but just as false cover story would be leaked to the more determined members of the media to make them feel like they'd got to the bottom of things like the hard-nosed investigative journalists they were. And then it would all blow over. It happened all the time.

My arm was starting to ache now and I wished I'd thought to ask the Norforce medic for some aspirin before he left. The Walther was still around my neck and not knowing what was left in the magazine, I flipped the fire selector to single. Gordon looked like he was going to say something else and then changed his mind.

'You've got some of that non-dairy creamer crap on your face,' I said, touching my lip.

He nodded vacantly. When he glanced down to look for a paper napkin I shot him. Just once, in the face, right between the eyes. It's not something I'd usually do.

ACKNOWLEDGEMENTS

I would like to thank everyone at Penguin, especially Bob Sessions, publishing director, and Clare Forster, my publisher, for their continued support; designer Debra Billson for the look of the book; Rod Morrison for his input; and senior editor Belinda Byrne for her warmth, good humour and guidance in shepherding the book so smoothly through the editing process. And last, but never least, my agent Selwa Anthony, for her sage advice, wise counsel and consummate negotiating skills.